CHAPTER 1

I heard the car pull into the driveway before it even came to a stop. That was saying something since my now ex-husband was driving a four-year-old Prius instead of his Tesla.

Since becoming a vampire, all my senses were becoming sharper and more focused.

I chugged down my tumbler of O-positive blood and quickly washed the cup out before sticking it into the dishwasher. Khalan, my vampire Maker and all-around pain in my ass, had been leaving a cooler of blood at the foot of my bed once a week. After he had turned me into a vampire, I had resisted drinking from hapless humans, except for a slip-up or two, and had existed on animal blood instead. Khalan hated that. He would rather I take human blood than drink animal blood. He was an animal lover and despised all humanity. But now that my source for animal blood was no longer an option, I turned a blind eye to whoever Khalan had attacked to bring me my food.

I guess he figured as long as he delivered it, I wouldn't question who he'd gotten it from. I had been keeping a close

1

eye on the local news for dead bodies drained of blood. But none had popped up on my radar. Yet.

The doorbell rang just as I was heading into the living room.

I unlocked the door and saw my two beautiful children standing there with their backpacks. My ex-husband, Miles, stood behind them with a fixed smile on his face.

"Hey, girls." I bent, and Gabby ran into my arms. I hugged her tightly. I noticed that her hair had not been brushed and smelled a little funky. I looked at my eldest, Arianna, over Gabby's shoulder. She was busy studying the welcome mat, but at least her hair was brushed, and I could tell from where I stood that she didn't smell.

"Hey, sweetie." I brushed my hand over Arianna's dark hair. She was getting older and hated for me to hug her. Teenage years were the worst.

She gave me a smile and a side-hug. My heart soared at the affectionate touch. It was more than I had expected.

"Did you guys have fun at Daddy's?" I looked between them.

Arianna huffed and dropped her bag by the door before walking toward the kitchen.

"Sure did." Gabby smiled. "Daddy ran out of toothpaste and tried to make us use some baking soda, but Arianna said she'd rather die. Then she saw a giant cockroach the size of my big toe and screamed. She jumped on the counter and wouldn't come down for half an hour. Until I squashed it with one of Daddy's medical books." Gabby's face was lit up like the Fourth of July as she'd recanted the tale.

I blinked and looked up at Miles.

Really looked at him.

He had lost more weight than I realized since our divorce. His hair was starting to gray around the temples, and tiny lines had cropped up around the corners of his blue eyes. His shoulders were slightly hunched as if he were carrying the guilt of what he'd done to our family and marriage.

The anger and hurt of his infidelity were still alive inside me, but it didn't burn as brightly as it once had.

"Why don't you go get a shower and brush your teeth." I looked down at Gabby.

Her face fell as if I had taken away her favorite toy.

"And then I'll make dinner."

I watched as she headed in the direction of her room, hoping she would use a liberal amount of shampoo when she washed her hair. I made a mental note to give her hair a sniff test.

Gabby was my tomboy who didn't care a smidge for hygiene. She was the complete opposite of Arianna, who was blossoming into early womanhood and cared about looks and clothes and boys.

"I guess I should go." Miles dug his hand into his jeans' pocket and pulled out a folded check. "Sorry it's a little late. I was waiting until I got paid for my extra shifts in the ER."

I frowned in confusion and took the check from his outstretched hand. "But you already paid your child support for the month."

"This is the alimony check." He shoved his hands back into his jeans' pockets.

My gut curled into a tight ball, courtesy of the guilt that had just been dumped inside my stomach.

"Oh," I said softly.

When we had been trying to mediate our divorce, Miles had accused me of basically being an unfit mother, which he'd heard from my arch nemesis, Veronica Counts. She'd lied to cause dissension between me and Miles during our mediation. She was evil to her core. To add insult to injury, someone had also been trying to kill me during that time. I had been poisoned, hit in the head with a shovel, pinned to

3

the ground by my garage door, and my brake lines had been cut.

I had thought it was Miles. In my anger, I'd used my vampiric power of glamour on him and forced him to agree to give me the house, a large amount of child support, and an even more obscene sum of alimony.

After he'd agreed to all my terms, I'd learned that it wasn't Miles trying to kill me, but my former BFF's soon-to-be ex-husband, Brad Stollings, who was trying to do the deed. He had known that his wife, my ex-friend Nikki, was having an affair with Miles. He'd kept his mouth shut because he didn't want Nikki to leave him for Miles. When I demanded a divorce from Miles, Nikki didn't let her shirt touch her back before leaving Brad.

In his twisted, deranged brain, Brad blamed me for the demise of his marriage. He'd said I should have just kept quiet and "settled for breadcrumbs."

But that wasn't who I was or would ever be. I couldn't be a woman who settled for a nice house while my husband cheated on me. I wasn't built like that.

"You want to come in for something to drink? We could chat about the girls."

His eyes brightened a little, and he rubbed the back of his head. "Coffee would be great."

"Come on in the kitchen." I waved him inside and shut the door.

My designer flats barely made a noise as I walked through the house. He eased into one of the stools at the bar. "Are you sure you want coffee? I have a nice bottle of Pinot Noir that Gina gave me."

"No. Coffee is fine. I have to pick up a shift tonight in the ER tonight."

I went to the gourmet coffee machine and started making a cup. At the refrigerator, I pulled out creamer and set it in front of Miles. I didn't drink creamer, but I kept it around for my friends when they dropped by.

"Is one of the doctors out sick? Is that why you're working in the ER?" I pulled the freshly brewed cup of coffee out from under the drip and placed it in front of him.

"No. I'm having a little trouble paying my bills on time." He stirred creamer into his coffee until it was a pretty shade of caramel.

Guilt gnawed at my vampire heart.

Guess I wasn't that cold, unfeeling creature after all.

"Are you still living in that condo?" When we separated, Miles had leased and then bought a condo in town. It was large and located on Main Street above the restaurants and art galleries in our small town of Charming, Mississippi. It was gorgeous and also the perfect bachelor pad.

"No." He took a quick sip of his coffee and ducked his head. "I'm renting it out to some college kids for the summer."

"So, where are you staying?" I narrowed my eyes. He was supposed to tell me if he ever changed residence, as stated in our custody agreement.

"I'm renting a room at Mrs. Grishom's." He averted his eyes and took another sip.

"Mrs. Grishom? The old lady who lives in that Victorian house?" My eyes widened.

Mrs. Grishom was an old maid. She had to be close to ninety years old. She went to our church, First Baptist of Charming, and everyone made sure never to eat any casserole she made. She had about twenty cats, all inside, and she was a hoarder.

"Are you crazy? You can't stay in that house! And you sure can't let the girls stay there." I narrowed my eyes at him.

"Oh, don't worry. I'm not staying inside the house. I'm

5

staying in the apartment above the garage. She's letting me rent there for pretty cheap." He nodded.

"How many cockroaches have you seen since moving in?" I propped my hands on my hips.

"I sprayed it before I moved in." He lifted his chin.

"Yet Arianna saw one this weekend."

He rubbed the back of his neck and averted his eyes.

I wanted to stay mad, but he looked pitiful.

"Miles, how many extra shifts are you working?" I asked softly.

"I usually fill in at the ER after I'm finished doing surgery. The only time I don't is when I'm on call."

I sighed. "And when was the last time you had a day off?"

"I don't work when it's my weekend with the girls."

"And that's it? Miles, you look exhausted. You don't need to work this much."

"I can't afford *not* to. I'm hoping to make a little extra money by renting out the condo, and plan to move back in September. This is only temporary." He forked his fingers through his hair and looked at me.

"A lot can happen between now and then." I was the authority on that subject. In one night, my whole life had changed. I'd found out about Miles' affair right before being turned into a reluctant vampire.

His phone buzzed, and he pulled it out of his pocket.

His face fell. "It's the hospital. I have to go." He drained the mug and set it down on the kitchen island. "Thanks for the coffee."

"Just go out the garage." I opened the kitchen door and hit the button.

He stepped into the space. "Liking the new car?" He motioned to my black Volvo.

"It's not really that new." I had gotten it after my white

Volvo was totaled after my brakes had been cut. I had chosen the same model, just in a different color.

I glanced over at his Prius. "Why are you driving a Prius instead of the Tesla?"

His face burned bright red. "It's good on gas."

"Did you sell your Tesla?" Miles loved that car more than anything.

"I didn't have a chance. They repossessed it." He studied the ground. "The Prius isn't bad."

Despite all the shit he had put me through, I couldn't help but feel bad for the guy. Miles always took pride in appearances and, right now, the town of Charming probably thought he looked like a loser. He'd gone from riches to rags.

"I'll talk to my lawyer tomorrow and see about reducing the alimony."

"Rachel, even if you did, it would take months for it to be official." He gave me a sad smile and opened the car door.

"Miles." I held up the alimony check. "Why don't you take this back?" I had some money saved that I could live on until I could find some kind of job.

"I can't. It's the law. I can't afford to go to jail. What would the town think?" He slid into the Prius and drove silently down the hill.

He was in this financial bind because I had glamoured him into paying me so much. I had to figure a way out of it. If for nothing else, I needed to do it for my girls. I could not stomach the idea of them spending their weekends with their father in a cockroach-infested apartment over Mrs. Grishom's garage.

They deserved better.

CHAPTER 2

"Y̶ou want to decrease your alimony? Are you fucking nuts?" Cherry Cobbledick, my divorce attorney, nearly growled at me through the phone.

She hadn't been my first choice when I was trying to find a lawyer—mainly due to her absurd last name. I had originally gone with her partner Ben Over but he'd left me high and dry when he forgot a meeting. Thankfully Cherry came to the rescue and completed my divorce paperwork. As much as I hated her last name, she was the best, and she was a bulldog in the courtroom.

"Mile's is having a hard time paying child support and alimony." I rubbed my temple and yawned. It was a sunny July day, and the girls were playing in the pool. It was hard for me to stay awake during the day because the sun drained me so much. I preferred to stay under the umbrella with my cover up on and my new wide brimmed hat that looked like something from out of a black and white movie in an attempt to stay out of direct sunlight. Not to mention I had to drink twice as much blood to reenergize myself.

"Well, he should have thought about that before he put his dick in your best friend," Cherry snarked.

"Ex-best friend," I reminded her. Cherry was known for telling it like it is.

"Let me give you some advice, Rachel." Cherry took a deep breath. "Every day, I go to court to battle for the rights of ex-wives to get a fraction of what you managed to talk your ex-husband into handing over to you. I'm still not sure how you did it, but I have a mind to give you a job as a mediator just to give my clients an edge. And you want to lessen the financial burden on him? I don't think so. Besides, you have no job, no gainful employment experience, and no way to pay bills. You need this alimony more than anyone else." Cherry ended the call without so much as a goodbye.

I scowled at my new cell phone in my hand. I hated being hung up on. And I loathed being wrong.

I looked over at my girls. Arianna was sitting on the edge of the pool, looking a bit dejected.

She'd seemed sad since coming home from her dad's.

"Arianna, come over and let me put some more sunblock on you." I settled back in the lounge chair. The only reason I was outside was to watch the girls in the pool. Not to get a tan. Those days were long gone.

Arianna slowly walked toward me. I moved my legs over for her to perch on my lounger. She sat and gave me her back.

I sat up and squeezed a large amount of sunblock into my palms and then rubbed it on her slim shoulders. "Having a good summer?"

"I guess," she said, looking down.

"I know you were looking forward to spending a week with your dad. But he called early this morning and said he needed to reschedule. He has to work some overtime."

She sighed. "Can I tell you something?" She looked at me over her shoulder.

"Of course, honey." I finished lathering her back. She turned and faced me.

"Don't tell Dad, but I'm glad we don't have to go over there for a week." She bit her lip.

"Why is that, Arianna?" I asked softly. "Is it because of the apartment he's renting?"

"It's not just that. I mean, that place is gross, but it wouldn't matter if Dad didn't seem so..."

"So what?" I leaned in farther.

"I don't know. Depressed, I guess. He's not happy anymore." She shrugged.

My heart ached for my girl. I had to do something. Mile's situation was now affecting my children.

"Maybe I can help," I said softly.

Her eyes widened. "Are you two getting back together?"

"No, honey. I'm afraid not."

Her face fell.

"I think Daddy's stressed about money. I've been thinking about getting a job."

She blinked. "You? Get a job?"

"I used to work when your dad was going through medical school, Arianna. I was a secretary." I scowled.

"I don't know if that's a good idea." She looked away. "I mean, who's going to pick us up after school and take us to practice? Who's going to take care of us if you are working all the time?"

"I will. I'm sure I can find a job with hours that will fit around your school schedule." I tucked a dark strand behind her ear. "Look, I don't want you to worry about Daddy. I think things will work out in the end. They always do."

She got up and went back into the pool. This time, she

splashed her sister. This started a water war, and by the time it was over, they were both smiling.

That night, long after the girls had gone to bed, I pulled out my laptop. I headed into the living room and relaxed on the couch.

The hair on the back of my neck stood at attention. Something wasn't right. I turned to the French doors leading out to the back yard.

Staring back at me was two hundred and fifty pounds of vampire. Khalan, my Maker.

"What the hell are you doing here? You could have given me a heart attack."

He was already opening and walking through the French doors before I could stand.

"I brought you some dinner." He held up a cooler bag.

My mouth watered at the thought of blood. The sun had drained me more than I wanted to admit. Summer was hard on me as a vampire.

I took the cooler and nodded. "Thanks."

"That's the last time I'm delivering blood to you." He stared at me.

"But…"

"Rachel. You know you have to learn how to feed yourself. I may not always be around to help you." He forked his fingers through his hair.

"Well, what else are you going to do? Did you decide to go on vacation or something?" I frowned. "Is there a place for vampires *to* vacation?"

"Yes. And it's exclusive. You're not invited." Khalan snarked.

"Whatever." I walked into the kitchen and pulled out the tumblers of warm blood. "I hope this donor is still…"

"Alive?"

I turned and faced him. "Is he?"

11

"I guess you'll have to start going with me to find out."

I sat the cooler down on the kitchen island and gave him my full attention. "No, really. Are you going somewhere?"

"Yes."

"Where?"

"None of your concern." He looked at the tumblers of blood. "You need to go with me to feed. You need to learn how to control yourself so you don't end up killing someone."

"One murderer on the block is enough." I sighed.

My neighbor Cal had killed a college student a few months back. He was currently in jail awaiting trial. His wife, Carla, now delivered pizzas on the weekend to try and make ends meet.

I didn't want to end up like Carla, depending on someone else to pay the bills. And I certainly didn't want to deliver pizzas for a living.

"I'll go." I looked up at Khalan.

"Is this a trick?" He narrowed his eyes.

"No. I'm serious. I'll go. You're right." I swallowed after forcing the words out of my mouth. "I need to be more independent."

He stepped into my personal space and stared into my eyes.

My stomach warmed, and his scent washed over me.

I needed to step away, but I couldn't make my body obey me.

"You smell different. You smell…" I closed my eyes and inhaled deeply.

"How do I smell?" His deep voice sent a thrill straight through me.

My heart jack-hammered in my chest, and I tried to slow down my breathing.

He smelled good. Better than good. But he didn't need to

know that. When he first turned me, he'd smelled awful, a combination of skunk and cat pee. We had not exactly become the best of friends. He thought I was selfish, and I thought he was indifferent. But over the months, he'd saved my ass more than once, and he'd proven himself. He had done more for me than my cheating ex-husband, who was now living in the equivalent of a roach motel.

And then there was that one episode where Khalan and I had felt each other up and rolled around in bed like a couple of horny college students. But I had written that off as me needing to have a nervous breakdown over my ruined marriage, not that I was actually attracted to Khalan or anything.

I opened my eyes. He was so close. His breath caressed my cheek, and my lips parted. He leaned in, and I held my breath, waiting for him to kiss me.

"You need to put your blood in the refrigerator before it spoils." He stepped back.

I swallowed my frustration. "Thanks for this. Let me know next time you go *hunting*, and I'll go with you."

A slow smile curled his lips. "Think you got what it takes?"

I lifted my chin. "I know I have what it takes."

He left out the back door without a goodbye.

I groaned. What the hell was wrong with me wanting Khalan to kiss me?

"I need a date. That's what I need. Or just a booty call to get all this sexual frustration out of my system."

But I had other, more important things to do first. Like, get a job to support my children and me.

CHAPTER 3

*S*ummer vacation had finally ended, and I was ready for the girls to get back in school. Arianna was entering tenth grade, and Gabriella was starting sixth.

While they were a week into the new school year, I was one week into my new job as a barista at the local coffee shop, Caffeine and Cookies.

"Mrs. Jones, you put in the vanilla flavor instead of the caramel. Again." Max Rainey held up the coffee cup. He had been making my coffee for years, and I was a regular at the coffee shop. When I applied, I hadn't let anyone know that I was working. It wasn't that I was ashamed of getting a job, it was more worry for what my friends would say in response to me getting a job to lessen the burden on Miles.

I still had the alimony check in the top drawer of my dresser. Just in case. I wasn't a big enough fool to tear up a check until I was sure the job at Caffeine and Cookies would work out.

"Sorry. I thought I put the right flavor in this time." I stifled a yawn behind my hand. I had applied for multiple jobs online, but the only one that had gotten back to me was the coffee shop.

It was a perfect fit. I could work the shift after I took the girls to school and be off in time to pick them up. I kept my own steel tumbler of warmed blood nearby to get me through the day. The pay was better than I'd expected and the job came with benefits—not that I would need them since I was a vampire, and the girls were covered under Miles' insurance.

The job should have been easy, except I couldn't keep up with the fast pace and the different ways to make a cup of fancy coffee.

Max forked his fingers through his hair and looked out the window. His eyes widened. "It looks like we're about to get busy."

I followed his gaze out the window. Five cars full of college students had pulled into the parking lot and piled out of the vehicles.

"How do you feel about running the register while I make the coffees?" He gave me an uncertain look.

Truth be told, I liked the register better than making the drinks. "I can handle it." I gave him a smile and a confident nod.

The door opened, and the noise level rose dramatically inside the tiny shop.

"Hi, welcome to Caffeine and Cookies Coffee Shop. Can I take your order?" I asked the guy with blond hair and blue eyes who stepped up to the register.

He gave me an easy grin and leaned on the counter. "You sure can, sweetheart. My name is Todd."

I resisted the urge to write Turd on the cup and ignored his attempt at flirting. "What can I get for you, Todd?"

"Your number." He grinned.

The girl behind him narrowed her eyes at me and sighed loudly. "Hurry up, Todd. We don't have time for this shit."

"Easy, Helen. Be nice." Todd grinned.

"What will it be, Todd?" I gave him a dead stare.

"I want one of those peppermint crunch lattes."

I looked over at Max. He shook his head.

"I'm sorry. That's a seasonal drink. We only have them at Christmas."

He sighed, and the smile slid off his face. "Well, that's the only thing I ever order."

"So you only go to the coffee shop at Christmas?" If Todd was the future of our world, we were all in a lot of trouble.

"Yeah." He shrugged.

"Hurry the fuck up, Todd. We have to be on the road in ten minutes." A big guy with muscles and a letterman jacket yelled behind the troublesome customer.

"They don't have the peppermint crunch latte." He turned and addressed his friends.

"Then get something else," one of the girls yelled.

"I don't know what to get. It's the only thing I ever get." He crinkled his brow as he read over the menu behind the counter.

Helen finally got fed up waiting and elbowed her way to the front of the line. "Then let everyone else order while someone reads the menu to you."

Todd glared but didn't say a word.

"Welcome to Caffeine and Cookies. What's your name, and what would you like?" I asked pleasantly.

"Helen. I'll have a tall skinny vanilla latte with extra whipped cream, five small cappuccinos, two small espressos with a shot of vanilla in one and caramel in the other. I also need seven small coffees, one regular, and leave room for cream on each one. Oh, and five of the chocolate chip cookies, two brownies, and fifteen sugar cookies."

I froze. "I'm sorry. Can you repeat that, slowly?" I felt a bead of sweat roll down my neck. "And I didn't get the names for the different coffees for the cups. Or did you want all of them labeled *Helen?*"

"Are you stupid or something." She cringed.

"Rachel, hurry up and put the order into the computer so I can start making the drinks," Max whispered loudly.

I turned to face him and glared. "She ordered about a hundred coffees with no name on any of them."

"What's the issue?" Helen propped her hands on the counter and leaned in. "Are you having problems doing your job?"

Max slid in front of me and faced the girl and gave her a smile. "No, she's just…"

"I think she's not smart enough to get a simple coffee order right." Helen crossed her arms over her chest. "I don't have time to sit around and wait until some idiot learns how to use a cash register and write names on paper cups."

Anger flared in my body like a rocket on the Fourth of July. I could feel my body heat with it and had no way to stop it. "Excuse me, what did you call me?" I shoved Max out of my way so I could see Helen head-on.

"Idiot. I called you an idiot." She cringed. "Can you not hear either?"

I reached across the counter and grabbed her scrawny wrist.

"Hey, let go of me!" Her eyes widened.

"Let me tell you something, you entitled brat. There are people in this world that aren't as fortunate as you to have rich, overindulgent parents. They aren't handed everything on a silver platter. Those people have to work for a living. Those people are giving back to the world in ways you never will. And if I ever come across you being rude and arrogant to one of those hard-working people, I swear I will put my size six shoe up your little ass."

"Rachel!" Max's voice brought me back to reality. I wasn't sure if it was the hysteria of his tone or how silent the entire room had gotten.

I let go of Helen's arm and looked around. All the college students were mute and staring at me.

"Rachel." Max's voice was low but stern. "I need to see you in the back."

I followed him back to the tiny storeroom that housed the extra supply of coffee cups and large bags of coffee beans. The beat of my heart began to slow, and the white noise between my ears started to fade.

He looked at me with his puppy dog brown eyes and said the words I didn't need to hear.

"I'm sorry, Rachel. But you're fired."

CHAPTER 4

"*H*ow in the world did you manage to get fired from the coffee shop? Wasn't that an easy job?" Gina blinked at me over her glass of wine. I'd called her that night to come over so I could vent a little.

I liked Gina. She never gossiped, and she pretty much stayed in her lane. She was a businesswoman, respected, and an athlete. She had run the Boston Marathon at least three times that I knew of.

"I didn't call you over here to make me feel even worse." I flopped back on the couch and stared at my tall ceilings.

"Why *did* you call me, Rachel?" Gina set her wine glass down on the end table and rested her elbows on her knees. "I would have thought you'd call Liz."

I sat up and looked at Gina. "I'm going to be honest. You are very independent despite being married. You're gorgeous. Talented. Smart. Plus, you never gossip about anyone. I love that about you."

A small smile graced her lips. "Thank you, Rachel. That means a lot. I kind of think people assume I'm a hard-ass because I don't engage in gossip. It's almost anti-Southern."

She eased back on the couch and picked up her glass once more. "Remind me again why you're even working when we all know that you took Miles to the cleaners in the divorce. Congrats, by the way." She toasted me with her wine.

I grabbed a throw pillow and held it over my face. "Ugh." When I pulled it away, I looked at her. "How do you know how much I ended up getting anyway?"

"No one knows for certain. All anyone is saying is that Miles is living above Ms. Grishom's garage in an apartment, working extra shifts in the ER, and driving a Prius." She shrugged. "I would have to say that driving a Prius was a big red flag that Miles is broke."

I let out a shaky laugh. I took another drink of my Merlot and looked at her. "What if I told you I feel guilty about all of that. And now I'm trying to find a job so Miles doesn't have to pay so much alimony."

"Why would you do that?" Gina gave me a horrified look. "He's the one who cheated on you. With your best friend, no less. He was arrogant enough to think he could have his cake and eat it, too. That asshole should pay."

"That's true." I worried my fingernail between my teeth and looked at her. "But he is still the girls' father. And it's affecting them by how depressed and worn out he is. I'm trying to do right by my children." I sighed heavily and stared at my friend.

"Rachel Jones. You are one of the few classy women I know." Gina lifted her glass in the air and toasted me before drinking.

"I don't feel like it."

"But you are. Trust me."

Her words warmed my heart and made me smile. It had been a while since I'd been complimented on my character. I seemed to have lost some self-respect and courage along the road to getting a divorce.

I wanted to reclaim those things.

"Thank you, Gina. I needed to hear that."

"What you *need* to do is tell me who's doing your Botox." She gave me a sly grin. "You look younger every day."

I couldn't tell her it wasn't Botox. A perk of becoming a vampire was that it erased any signs of aging. Instead of my late thirties, I looked to be in my twenties.

I let out a laugh. Her grin faltered, and she huffed. "Fine. But one of these days, I'm going to find out who it is."

"In the meantime, I need a favor," I said.

"What do you need?"

"A job. Do you know of anyone who needs a secretary?" I asked hopefully.

"Off the top of my head, no. Secretarial jobs are hard to come by. But let me ask around."

"Don't tell anyone you're asking for me. I'd rather not have to explain why I'm looking for a job." I gave her a sheepish grin.

"I'll be discrete." She nodded.

"And it doesn't have to be a secretarial job, although that's the only experience I've ever had. I did that while Miles went to med school. Ideally, I would like a job where I can work around the girls' schedules and make a lot of money."

Gina laughed and shook her head. "Right. The only thing that pays a lot of money is with Liz's odd Uncle Stan."

"Uncle Stan? You mean that private investigator?"

"Yeah. He just fired one of his workers. He was supposed to be hiding in the closet to take photos of his client's wife and her lover. The wife discovered him, and *they* ended up having sex on the closet floor instead. The husband found them."

"Damn."

"Yeah. Not only did he not get any photos, the husband fired Uncle Stan." Gina shook her head. "Can you imagine

21

having a job like that where you get paid an extravagant amount of money to photograph people having sex?"

"Extravagant amount of money? It can't pay that much." An urgency like I had never known gnawed in my gut. I had the overwhelming urge to call up Uncle Stan immediately.

"The photographer was getting a couple thousand a night for a stakeout. And an extra thousand on top of that when he got photos."

"Geez, if he worked every night, even without getting any photos, that's twelve thousand for a seven-day week."

"I know. But that's not a job for you. There would be no way for you to work all night and take the kids to school and then pick them up." Gina shook her head. "You should write up your resume and post it on that temp site. Sometimes, a temporary job turns into a permanent position if you do a good job." She shrugged

"That's a good idea. I hadn't thought of that. Thanks, Gina."

Later after Gina had left, I went to my laptop and pulled up the temp site that serviced the Charming, Mississippi city and surrounding areas. I made myself look at all the jobs, despite wanting to look up Uncle Stan and his private investigation agency.

"That job's not for you." Gina's words kept popping up in my mind, making me feel guilty for even entertaining the idea. Instead, I continued typing in search words for the temp site.

A flood of job postings popped up.

There were plenty of night positions for cashiers at all of the gas stations, but that wasn't the type of job I wanted. It barely paid minimum wage.

I kept looking.

There were teacher's aide positions at the girls' school, but I knew that didn't pay very much either.

There was a listing at a car lot, but the hours were long, and it wouldn't allow me to pick up the girls from school.

I kept scrolling.

Around two in the morning when my resolve had waned and the lure of twelve thousand dollars a week was too much for me to resist, my fingers typed in private investigation agencies in Charming Mississippi.

Only one came up.

DISCRETE P.I. AGENCY leapt from my screen.

There wasn't a website, just a number and an address. I jotted the number into my cell phone's contacts.

I closed my computer, excited that maybe, just maybe I had found a job that would work around my life.

After I had dropped the girls off at school, I would call Liz's Uncle Stan and try to set up an interview. I just hoped and prayed that he hadn't hired anyone yet.

CHAPTER 5

I parked my Volvo in the parking lot behind one of the large office buildings on Main Street. I had just dropped off the kids at school. Five minutes ago, I had called Uncle Stan to inquire about the job opening, and he'd told me to come over so we could talk. He'd said that he had another person coming to interview, as well. I didn't have time to change clothes, so I drove over wearing my black skinny jeans, white and gold sneakers, and a short-sleeved white blouse with a picture of a large white rose splattered across the top.

I looked in my visor mirror. I didn't have any makeup on. I was kind of worried that my fresh-faced look would discourage Uncle Stan from considering me a real candidate for the job. If I had known I was going to interview today, I would have come in full makeup, high heels, and a black pantsuit. I wanted Stan to know that I was serious about the job. I knew how important first impressions were.

I dug around in my purse until I found a tube of lipstick. I swiped some Pretty Pink Berries onto my lips and pressed them together. It was the best I could do on short notice.

I made my way to the front of the building and opened the front door. DISCRETE P.I. AGENCY was located on the top level of the old building. The first floor housed a woman's boutique and hair salon. The second level was an accounting service. The third floor held one of the less-than-stellar law firms in Charming, which seemed to lose every case for every client they ever had.

When the elevator dinged for the fourth floor, I tried to calm my racing heart before the doors opened.

I stepped out into a dark hall. It was long with only a glass door at the end. Mildew and dust hung heavily in the air, and the old wood floor creaked with every step I took.

I stopped at the door and reached for the knob. I turned and had to give the door a shove with my shoulder to get it to budge.

It finally gave, creaking as it came unstuck and swung open.

An old, metal desk piled high with paperwork was the first thing I saw. The chair behind it was empty.

"Hello?" My voice echoed in the room.

"Back here." The gruff male voice came from a room off to the right. I followed the sound with trepidation.

Was I more worried about not getting the job or getting hired? I couldn't decide.

I stepped inside a small space that barely had enough room for a desk. Standing behind the crowded surface was the man I recognized as Liz's uncle, Stan. He was short and bald with a large, round belly. His glasses rode low on the end of his nose, and he scowled as he went through the scattered paperwork on his desk.

"I don't know if you remember me, but I'm Liz's friend. Rachel Jones. We met at her cookout last summer." I held out my hand.

He barely gave me a glance before grasping my fingers.

"This whole damn place is in a tumble. Had a break-in last night."

"Here? Did they steal anything?"

"Ha! Nothing important." He spared me a grin. I noticed he was missing a front tooth.

"Did you call the police?" I clasped my hands together, scared to disturb the crime scene.

"Police? Why the hell would I do that? Hell, I got incriminating photos of the police chief and the mayor. The cops are the last people I would call." Stan huffed and sat down in his chair. "Sit." He waved me to the chair across from him.

I eased into the seat. I noticed how he narrowed his eyes as he assessed my outfit.

"You look like a soccer mom."

"I *am* a soccer mom." I looked down at my casual attire. "I would have changed before coming into the interview, but I didn't have time to run home."

He cocked his head at me. "So, you are interested in working for my agency?"

"Yes, sir." I took a deep breath. "You see, I'm recently divorced…"

He held up his hand. "Yes. I already know all about that."

"You do?" I shifted in my seat.

He gave me a look. "Charming is a small town, and in the line of business I'm in, I know everything that goes on with everyone." He nodded at me. "Your husband is that doctor that cheated on you with your best friend. The blonde with the nice ass."

I pressed my lips into a thin line. I hated that everyone I came across thought Nikki had a nice ass. "Her ass isn't that nice."

He stared silently.

"Anyway, I need a job to support my girls. But since I've not worked in years, it's been hard to find the right fit."

"So, what you mean is that you want to make a lot of money and work around your schedule with your children." He narrowed his assessing eyes on me again. "How many kids you got?"

"Two. They are in school."

He relaxed a little and leaned back in his chair. "Mrs. Jones, do you know exactly what I am looking for in a photographer? I mean, it's not taking family photos in an outdoor setting. This may not be a good fit for you."

"Mr...."

"Call me Uncle Stan. I don't need anyone getting formal by calling me *mister*."

"Uncle Stan. I understand what this job entails. It involves taking compromising photos of people in Charming. Some of which I know."

"Exactly. And it requires someone to blend into their environment without sticking out."

"I can do that. I can blend."

"Can you stay professional?"

"Of course."

"What I'm asking is...can you do your job without letting your emotions or your ethics get in the way? Would you be able to get pictures of one of your friends who was committing an indecent act and turn them over to me?"

"I doubt that anyone I knew would be doing anything that would require a private investigator. My friends are pretty boring."

Uncle Stan arched an eyebrow.

Miles' affair flashed through my mind. I shoved it away and fidgeted in my seat.

"What about photography? Are you going to be able to wait for hours until you get the right photo? Are you going to be able to take pictures of some high-powered politician getting an eggplant shoved up his ass by a hooker?"

I cringed. "That's actually a thing?"

"More than you know." He nodded solemnly.

"Look, I can do the job. I really can. I'd prefer to blend in, actually. I don't want anyone to know I'm doing this."

"Good, because if I give you the job, you can't tell anyone. Not even your girls. If word gets out that you're my new photographer, people will run when they see you coming down the street."

"I understand. I will be completely discrete. Since I can work around my girls' schedules, they won't ever find out."

"What about nights? Can you work nights?"

I didn't hesitate. "Absolutely." I would figure something out once the girls went to bed. "Would it be every night? I'm just asking so my neighbors wouldn't get suspicious about me leaving every night. I'm usually a homebody."

"Not every night. Maybe two at the most. Some weeks no nights at all."

"I can get a babysitter. That should be fine." He opened a desk drawer and pulled out a camera. It looked pretty expensive. I had friends who were always taking their kids' pictures with their fancy cameras. To be honest, I could never justify spending that much on a camera when I could just take photos with my cell phone.

"How are you at taking photos?" He put the camera in front of me.

"Good," I lied.

"I'm going to hire you for a one-time job. See how you do, then decide from there."

My heart raced with relief. "Thank you. What do you need me to do?"

"I want you to follow this person today." He shoved a piece of paper across the desk. "Here is his address. He is supposed to be disabled. Says he's blind due to an automobile accident. If that's true, then he shouldn't be leaving his house."

I read the name on the paper. "Shannon Curtis. So, what makes you think he's not blind?"

"I pulled his monthly credit card bill. Seems he's watching a whole lot of internet porn for a blind man," Uncle Stan deadpanned.

"Maybe he's just listening." I shrugged.

"Maybe. But it's your job to stake out his house, even get close enough to get pictures of whatever he's doing inside. He's got a very tall fence around his back yard, and the last photographer couldn't get over it. I have a feeling something weird is going on."

I nodded and took the expensive-looking camera in my hand. "I've got some time today before I pick up the girls. I'll run home and change into something…"

"No!" He held up his hand. "Don't change your clothes. You look like a mom who has lost a dog. In fact, use that as your cover if people in the neighborhood ask you what you're doing."

I nodded. "Anything else?"

"Yeah. No matter what, don't blow your cover. Those pictures are going to be worth a lot of money."

"And if he's innocent?"

A slow smile crossed his lips. "Honey, they ain't ever innocent."

CHAPTER 6

$\mathcal{I}$ followed the address on my navigation system, which led me to a nice neighborhood on the other side of town. The community was small and cozy with large trees and well-manicured lawns. The homes were older, but you could tell the residents took great pains to keep their yards well-manicured and the houses had great curb appeal. It looked like a place retired people lived.

There were a lot of cars parked on the street. I decided to park one house down from Shannon's.

My heart nearly stopped when a woman opened the front door of the house I was parked in front of and trained her gaze on me. Making a quick decision, I grabbed the camera and got out of my car.

"Hi!" I waved and smiled as I walked toward her.

"I don't buy anything from solicitors." She narrowed her eyes. She was in her late sixties with slightly graying hair. She wore gray slacks and a pretty floral blouse with ballet slippers.

"Oh, I'm not selling anything." My smile was frozen on my face. I had to give her a name. "My name is Nikki

Stollings." I chose my ex-best friend because I hated her. "I'm just out looking to take some photos of the neighborhood. I work for the high school, and they are looking for places outside where we can have the senior portraits taken this year." I looked at her landscape and smiled. "I couldn't help but notice how beautiful your roses are. And the land-scaping is absolutely stunning. Did you have it profession-ally done?"

"No." She smiled widely. "I did it all myself. Me and my husband. My name is Betty Williams, by the way."

"Oh my, you certainly have an eye for it, Betty." I gently touched a light pink rose. "Do you mind if I get some photos of your flowers and the front of the house? I would love to show the school this place. And if your house is chosen, you will be credited when it goes into the yearbook."

"Oh, well, of course." She lifted her head and smiled, very pleased with herself.

"Now, Betty, I have to mention that we have a few more houses we are looking at before the school decides on the best outdoor scenes for the pictures. But I really think you have a great shot at winning."

"Thank you. I do love to keep my flowerbed and back yard pristine. It's almost like therapy for me." Betty lifted her chin, perfectly pleased with her gardening skills.

I held up the camera, waiting for her permission. "May I?"

"Go ahead and take some pictures. Anything to help the school. Would you like a cup of tea while you're working?"

"I would love a cup. Thank you so much." I turned and aimed my camera at the landscape near the garage. It looked like I was taking photos of Betty's roses, but in reality, I was getting some pictures of Shannon's open garage.

The woman disappeared inside, and I made my way to the edge of the house, closer to my intended target.

The door in Shannon's garage suddenly opened. I pointed

my camera down to the purple petunias that ran along the stone border and pretended to be taking a picture.

I strained my ears. The man inside the garage was opening the freezer, judging by the squeak.

"Oh, here you are." Betty held out a mug with a tea bag floating inside. "I didn't know what you wanted, so I didn't add anything."

"That's perfect. I like it without cream or sugar." I lifted the mug to my lips and took a sip.

"That's a perfect cup of tea."

Betty smiled and sipped from her own cup. "You know, if it's senior pictures you want, you need to come have a look at my back yard. I have a gazebo and a waterfall, as well as flowers and foliage."

"You do?" I jerked my head to her.

"Yes." She laughed. "Come on, I'll take you through the gate on the side."

I followed as she led me to the back yard. This was even better. If I could find some kind of way to get higher and see into Shannon's back yard, then maybe I could catch him doing something that indicated he wasn't blind.

"This is lovely." The back yard was filled with flowers of all colors in various flowerbeds. There was a waterfall with Koi fish. A very tall gazebo with a sitting area underneath sat near the corner of the fence.

Betty's phone buzzed, and she pulled it out of her pants' pocket.

"I'll leave you to it back here. I have some cupcakes that I have to get frosted before I run them over to the nursing home."

"Oh, how nice. Thank you so much for letting me take all these pictures. And I appreciate the cup of tea."

"You're so welcome. I'll just be inside if you have any more questions." She smiled and walked back into the house as she chatted happily on the phone. I watched her shadow move through the house. I noted that the kitchen was on the other end of the home away from the gazebo.

"Perfect." I sat the cup down on the concrete of the fish pond and made my way over to the gazebo. I snapped pictures as I went while trying to see over into Shannon's back yard.

When I was sure that Betty wasn't going to come back outside, I looped my camera strap around my neck and scaled the gazebo to get higher. At the top, I smiled. I had a vantage point. I could see over into Shannon's back yard.

Other than a grill and some outdoor furniture, it looked pretty empty. I thought I had lost all hope of getting any dirt on the man. Until he walked out into the yard.

He was wearing cut-off denim shorts and nothing else. I grimaced at the sight of his large stomach protruding over the shorts in an attempt to escape the tight confines.

He had sunglasses shoved on his head and a laptop computer in his hand. He walked over to the outdoor lounger and sat.

For someone who was blind, he sure was getting around well. But then again, maybe he had memorized his back yard.

I picked up my camera and held it to my eye. A wave of guilt washed over me. What if the guy really was blind? What if he really couldn't see? What kind of person would that make me?

His cell phone rang, and he dug it out of his back pocket.

He looked at the screen and then frowned before answering the call.

I cocked my head. If he were blind, he wouldn't be reading the cell phone screen.

I snapped another picture.

Shannon finally ended the call and tossed his phone on

the lounger. He opened his laptop and began typing on the keyboard.

I narrowed my eyes, trying to see if maybe, just maybe, the keyboard was Braille. I had no idea if that was even a thing, but I was still trying to be optimistic about the guy.

"What the fuck?" Shannon threw his sunglasses onto the patio and stood up.

I froze where I was perched on the gazebo. Had he seen me?

"I can't believe the assholes are trying to make me pay for porn. Porn is supposed to be free!" He gathered up his laptop and started typing like a man on a mission.

Why would a blind man need to pay for porn? Was he getting it just to hear the sex noises?

He growled and then reached for his back pocket. He dug out his wallet and pulled out a credit card. He sat down at the patio table. He looked from his credit card to the computer, typing in his credit card information.

I narrowed my eyes and snapped some photos.

A lot of photos.

Any guilt I had vanished with each snap of my camera.

"Nikki, what are you doing up there?" Betty's voice carried across the yard.

Shannon stopped what he was doing and jerked his head in my direction.

His gaze met mine. He glared at me. "What the hell are you doing with that camera?" he bellowed.

Shit, he'd seen me.

I quickly began my descent. My camera strap caught on one of the wooden pieces of the gazebo. The nylon tightened around my throat like a noose. My feet dangled in the air while I clawed at the vise-like strap across my neck, constricting my breathing.

Panic swelled in my body. I had to do something.

I grabbed one of the wooden beams and hoisted myself up then slid my neck out of my noose. I grabbed the camera before landing on my feet.

"On my! Are you okay?" Betty pressed her hand to her heart. "I thought you were going to choke yourself."

"Oh, I'm fine." I gave her a smile. "I was just up there getting some wide shots of your backyard." I nodded in the direction of Shannon's house. "He scared me and I lost my balance."

"Hey, lady. What the hell are you doing? Trying to get a naked photo of me?" Shannon yelled across the fence.

Betty walked out into the back yard and eyed the fence. Shannon was banging on the wood as if attempting to scale the wall.

"Do you know him very well?" I asked.

"I don't associate with his *kind*." Betty pressed her lips into a thin line. "His poor mother died and left him that house. He does nothing all day but walk around half-naked and stay on that stupid computer."

"Do you think he's dangerous? I mean, it sounds like he's trying to come into your yard. Which is *your* property." My eyes darted back to the fence. I saw a hand reach the top and heard a lot of huffing and puffing.

"Mrs. Williams, I think we better get inside. Maybe call the police." I wrapped my arms around her slender shoulders and tried to steer her back to the house.

She knocked off my hand and glared at the fence. "Shannon Curtis, you better not tear that fence down. I will press charges."

"He seems very active for a guy who can't see," I muttered.

She spun around and leveled her glare at me. "That fool isn't blind. He's faking it."

My mouth dropped open. "Are you sure?"

She raised her voice so Shannon could hear everything

she said. "Of course, I'm sure. He's committing fraud against the insurance company, and I'm sick and tired of him and people like him not working for their money."

"You old hag. When I get over there, I'm going—" Shannon's words dropped off. He cursed and tumbled down, taking part of the fence with him.

"That will teach him." Betty lifted her chin and stormed back inside.

I grabbed my camera, snapped one more picture of Shannon with the fence on top of him, and raced back to my car.

CHAPTER 7

I headed back to Uncle Stan's office. He hooked up the camera to his printer and printed out some pictures I had taken.

"These are good. Real good." He nodded in appreciation. "I'm surprised you were able to look over into his back yard. Did you get a ladder or something?"

"I climbed a gazebo." I sat in the chair and yawned. Between being out in the sun and running away from a sociopath who was scamming an insurance company, I was drained.

Uncle Stan cocked his head and narrowed his eyes. "Did you break and enter the neighbor's back yard?"

"No. The neighbor that lives next to him, Betty Williams, let me in." I shrugged. "I told her I was scouting locations for senior pictures. She had a lovely front yard, and she offered to let me see the back yard, as well. She also confirmed that she didn't believe Shannon to be blind. In case your client wants to call her as a witness in court."

He let out a laugh. "That's some creative thinking right there. It's always important not to do anything illegal to obtain the pictures. Otherwise, they are not admissible in court."

He reached into the drawer and pulled out a cashbox. He opened it, counted out some bills, and slipped them into an envelope.

"I pay every time I get the photos. They always have to be quality. Nothing blurry or shaky or hard to make out. Those, I can't use." He slid the envelope over to me.

My eyes widened. "So, I got the job?" I picked up the envelope. I wanted to count the money but didn't want to be rude.

"As long as you deliver." He put the cash box back into the drawer and locked it. He grinned. "Go ahead. I know you want to count it." He arched his eyebrow.

I opened the envelope and thumbed through the wad of hundred-dollar bills.

"This is twelve hundred dollars." I looked up at him, amazed.

"Yep." He eased back into the chair and laced his fingers together over his stomach. "It won't always be the same amount. Just depends on the client and the job."

"I understand." I stuck the envelope into my purse.

He shoved the camera across the desk at me. "Keep this. You'll need it in a couple of days for the next job."

"What's the assignment?"

"It's a weird one." He eyed me.

"And this one wasn't?" I arched a brow.

"I have a client. She's a Seventh Day Adventist. She wants to divorce her husband but doesn't want to leave the church. Seventh Day Adventists don't look favorably on divorce. She wants to hire an escort to tempt her husband into committing adultery. I need you to get photos of them together so she can show them to the church elders and get approval for a divorce."

I shook my head. "She's willing to trap her husband with an escort to get a divorce? What do the Seventh Day Adventists have to say about that?"

"I don't know, and I don't give a damn. But she wants out of this marriage, and she's desperate," Uncle Stan stated. "You won't be needed until Friday. That's when all of this is going down."

"Does this pay as much as the insurance fraud?" I snorted.

He grinned. "Even more. You get the pictures, and I'll pay you three thousand dollars."

My smirk slid off my face. "Three thousand?"

"Yep. A desperate wife will do anything to get out of an unhappy marriage."

* * *

THAT NIGHT after the kids had gone to sleep, I sat up in bed. I had gathered all my financial statements and bills and spread them across the comforter. After looking over all the expenses, I realized that this job with Uncle Stan could be quite lucrative. If I made steady money, it would cover what Miles was paying me in spousal support, maybe even more. That is if I kept getting the photos.

"What are you doing?" Khalan asked from the doorway.

I steeled my expression. "You do realize this is a private residence, right?"

"And since you are my progeny, you have no privacy." He sneered.

I looked up from my task. "What do you want, Khalan? Here to remind me what a failure I am as a vampire?"

"Only if you're ditching your obligation to go hunting with me."

I narrowed my eyes. "Is that tonight?"

He gave me a dead stare.

"Fine." I stood and looked down at my black yoga pants and matching T-shirt. "Am I dressed appropriately, or do I need to change?"

"Come on." He turned and walked out of the room. I quickly found my Ugg boots and slipped them on without any socks.

I caught up with Khalan in the kitchen.

"So, am I driving again?" I reached for my purse and then stopped. "Wait, I forgot about Gabby and Arianna. I can't just leave them here by themselves."

"I already planned for that." He turned and nodded out the back door.

"It better not be a glamoured Carla. I have a real issue with making someone do something against their will."

"It's not Carla." He walked over to the door and opened it.

A very large German Shepard walked into my kitchen.

I jumped back and stifled a scream.

"What are you doing? You can't bring that in here." I backed up a few feet.

The dog walked over to me and sat. He cocked his head and stared at me.

"Does it bite?"

"Not unless you ask it to," Khalan snarked.

"Smartass." I kept my eyes glued to the dog. "What is it doing in my house? Is this your new roommate or something?"

"More like *your* new babysitter."

I jerked my head to Khalan. "Oh. Hell. No."

"What?"

"I'm not leaving my children alone with a fierce beast that can tear my children's throats out." I looked at him wide-eyed.

"You are such a drama queen." He sighed and sat down on the

stool at the kitchen island. He seemed to dwarf my kitchen and made the space shrink a few feet. "Besides, in all actuality, you are the bigger threat to your children if you don't get any blood."

I ignored his comment.

"You cannot be serious about having a dog babysit my kids."

"Of course, I am. Think of it like that dog that babysits in that fairy tale."

I blinked and let out a loud sigh. There was no way I was winning this fight. "What's this dog's name?"

"Killer."

I looked at Khalan, hard.

He grinned. He was messing with me.

"You're an ass."

"So you keep reminding me." He stood. "Hurry up and let's go." He walked to the door leading out to the garage. "It's fine. Killer knows how to protect your children."

"What if there's a fire?"

"Then Killer will get the kids out of the house and call 911."

"The dog knows how to use the phone?"

"The *dog* is smarter than most people. Now quit stalling and let's get going before all the good blood donors get drunk." He walked out into the garage.

I turned and looked at Killer.

I pointed my finger at him. "Now look, buster. You don't hurt my kids. Got it?"

The dog's head cocked to the side, and a string of drool gathered on one side of his mouth. He didn't blink but held my gaze.

"And don't let anyone else hurt them either. Okay?"

The dog stared at me until I blinked.

"Ugh." I grabbed my purse and followed Khalan outside.

"Just for the record, I have a bad feeling about this." I looked back at the house.

"Duly noted. Now, let's go." He walked down the driveway toward the street.

I followed and caught up to him. "I thought we were going to drive."

"And how would that look? You driving away from your house at midnight and leaving your kids all alone."

I hesitated and looked around my neighborhood.

"Don't worry. Everyone on your street is sleeping. Besides, no one will see you leaving in your car. I brought my own vehicle. It's parked at the corner."

He didn't stop walking, so he didn't see the daggers I shot at him.

The neighborhood was dark, the only illumination were the few security lights on the ends of the street. The houses were silent, sleeping giants among perfectly manicured lawns. To the casual visitor of our neighborhood, it probably looked pristine and the epitome of a perfect life.

But I knew how people hid behind their beautiful mansions and expensive cars. The whole thing was an illusion, and money couldn't buy happiness or pay for peace of mind.

I was an expert on both.

"So, what kind of vehicle did you bring? A horse and buggy?" I hurried to keep up with Khalan's long strides.

"More like a hog."

I stopped. "I'm not riding an animal. Geez, I wouldn't think you would either since you are such an animal lover."

He stopped at the corner of the street and pointed to a chromed-out motorcycle. "I meant this kind of hog."

My mouth hit the asphalt. "Where did you get that?"

"I stole it." Khalan took the keys out of the pocket of his black jeans and straddled the beast.

"You are such a smartass. I can't ever get a straight answer out of you." I walked over to the bike. It was big and black with lots of shiny silver. There was even a small seat behind Khalan's.

"You getting on, or are you walking?" He looked over his shoulder at me.

"I've never ridden a motorcycle before," I said.

"That doesn't surprise me. Miles was probably the only guy you ever had sex with, too."

I curled my fingers into fists. "You know nothing about me."

"Yeah? I know that you're too scared to get on the back of this bike."

I shook my head. I held onto his shoulders and climbed onto the seat behind him.

"Just so you know, I'm doing this of my own free will. Your reverse psychology won't work on me."

"Look, I don't care. This is not some long, drawn-out conversation. I'm hungry, and I want my dinner." He turned the key, and the bike growled to life.

I tightened my arms around his waist and pressed my head into his back. "I don't have a helmet!"

"Don't worry. You won't need it. If we wreck, it won't kill you. It will just hurt like a bitch. Remember, you're immortal." He took off from the curb and accelerated into the night.

CHAPTER 8

$\mathcal{W}$e sped into town. We didn't pass any traffic, but there were a few cars parked in the mall parking lot where a bunch of college students had gathered.

At least anyone I knew would be in bed by now, so there was little chance that they would recognize me on the back of the bike with some stranger.

Khalan slowed and turned down a side street that led to Main Street. There were no bars, and the restaurants would be closed by now.

He came to a stop in an empty parking lot in the back of a restaurant and killed the engine.

"What are we doing here? There's no one around." I slid off the back of the bike and looked at the empty town.

"There are always people around. You're just not looking hard enough." Khalan dismounted the bike with the grace of a panther. My heart sped up a bit at the sight of him.

I shook my head. Khalan was handsome in his grungy, disgruntled kind of way. But he was my Maker, and he'd not been very helpful when it came to teaching me the ways of being a vampire.

Compassion was definitely not his strong suit. I, on the other hand, was very empathetic. Which meant that we were definitely not a match when it came to anything romantic.

"Where are we going? Is there some kind of underground vampire club that lures humans to their deaths?" I looked around and then over at Khalan.

He stood there and stared at me.

"What?"

"You really need to stop watching vampire movies." He rolled his eyes.

"I didn't get it from a movie. I got it from a romance novel." I shrugged.

"Come on." He headed toward a business off Main Street. I quickly caught up.

Main Street did not have your typical small-town feel. Even though there were restaurants and law offices, there was also a tattoo shop and a liquor store. Second Central Baptist Church, the other large Baptist church in Charming, had attempted to get their members to sign a petition to stop the tattoo shop and liquor store from opening. It hadn't mattered. In the end, both the liquor store and the tattoo shop had opened for business. I had known they would because I knew too many Baptists who liked to drink. Myself included.

We walked down the street lit by business signs and street lamps. A guy came out of the tattoo shop and headed toward us. I kept my head down and let my long, dark hair curtain around my face. I couldn't take the chance that it was someone I knew.

Khalan stopped in front of the tattoo parlor and opened the door.

"Here? We are going to have—" I looked around to make sure we were alone. "—dinner here?"

"Yeah. Come on." He waved me through.

45

I stepped inside. I was surprised by the faint scent of ink hanging in the air. A young guy sat behind the counter looking at a comic. He barely looked up when we walked in.

"We just did our last customer. We are closing for the night," the guy said.

"Are you?" Khalan stepped up to the counter. The guy looked up. His eyes widened when he saw Khalan leaning over him. "You are getting off work and are going home. Don't forget to lock up behind you."

The guy didn't blink but obeyed Khalan's command. He stood with a glazed look in his brown eyes and walked over to the door. He flipped the sign to *Closed* and walked out of the building, locking the door behind him.

Khalan didn't wait for me but walked down the hallway. When he got to the back door, he reached for the doorknob.

"Wait. We're leaving? But we just got here?" I said. I was beginning to get very irritated with my Maker. I had better things to do than follow him around on a wild goose chase.

"We are going out into the alley. We go through the tattoo parlor just in case we are being followed." He didn't wait for me but walked through the door leading outside. He gently pushed me in front of him before he locked the door.

I hesitated a second and then followed him out. A guy stood in the shadows wearing a dark hood. He raised a hand in greeting at Khalan.

"Is that...?"

"Dinner?" Khalan looked at me over his shoulder. A slow, sinister grin grew on his face.

Khalan stopped a few feet away from the stranger wearing a leather trench coat with a hood.

"Master Khalan." The man shoved the hood away from his face and dipped his head in a bow. He was in his late forties with salt and pepper hair. His beer belly protruded over his black leather pants, and he smelled like cheap cologne. He licked the sweat that was gathering on his upper lip, and his wide-eyed gaze darted over me before landing on Khalan. "You brought a date?"

"Something like that." Khalan snorted.

"I'm Blayze. With a Y." He bowed before me.

"That's not his name. His name is Bill." Khalan cringed.

"But, Master, when I'm in this role, my name is Blayze." His eyes locked on Khalan with a mixture of fear and excitement. He shifted his weight, and his too tight pants made a squeaking sound.

Khalan just shook his head in disgust. He waved his hand at me and growled. "She is my dinner companion for the night. Just call her R.K."

I glared at him. Khalan had given me the nickname Road Kill after he'd turned me into a vampire. Now, the asshole had shortened it. He knew I hated it, which meant he used it frequently.

"Just call me Rachel." I took the guy's hand.

"Wow, she's beautiful, Master Khalan. You don't usually bring dates." Bill, err Blayze, looked at Khalan.

I arched my brow and wondered about Khalan's social life.

"Let's get started, shall we?" Khalan changed the conversation, and I stifled a grin.

"Yes, Master." Bill headed down the alley away from the glare of the security lights. I looked up and noticed that there were no cameras anywhere around.

"Where are we going? And why did Bill, or Blayze with a Y, call you 'Master?' I can tell he's human. Does he know what you are?" I whispered to Khalan.

"You ask a lot of questions." Khalan glanced over at me.

"I'm going to keep asking them, and a lot more if you don't tell me what's going on." I gritted my teeth.

"Bill calls me Master because he and his friends are part

of an underground group that likes to roleplay. They are the hapless humans who offer themselves up to me, and I am the evil vampire who drinks their blood."

"Are you fucking kidding me?" I stopped in my tracks.

Khalan stopped and glared at me.

"Bill knows you're a vampire? Do you know how bad this could be? This is a small town, for cripes' sake. Everyone will find out, and then they'll know what *I* am." I turned to walk away. Khalan grabbed my hand.

"I told you, it's roleplaying. They think I'm roleplaying, too." He leaned in close and lowered his voice. "After I take their blood, I glamour them. They don't remember me drinking from them. They only think we're acting out a game."

Bill stopped at the end of the alley and pulled out a key. He looked back at us. "Is everything okay, Master?"

I snorted. "I bet you love that."

"Him calling me Master?" Khalan shrugged. "I'd rather hear it from you."

I let out a bark of laughter and grabbed my stomach. "Good luck with that, sucker."

Khalan glared and walked toward Bill. After I composed myself, I followed.

CHAPTER 9

*W*e stepped inside the building. I was shocked to see people all dressed in different attire, milling around inside and chatting. The interior of the large room was awash with dim, red lights and billowing smoke from a hidden fog machine that wafted haze up from the floor in an attempt to make the room look dangerous. Candles of all sizes had been placed along the floor, making a trail to the bar on the far side of the room. Classical music played over the speakers.

I waved my hand in front of my face and coughed. "I wasn't expecting to see this many people. And why are they all dressed like they just came from a Renaissance Faire?" The smoke from the fog machine was making my eyes water.

"I already told you, it's a roleplaying group. Besides, they're not all dressed in period costumes." He nodded toward the end of the bar. A young, blond woman was dressed in a schoolgirl outfit with pigtails. She was sipping on a martini and studying the floor.

"Why am I not surprised?" I repressed a shiver and looked around the room for Bill—I mean Blayze.

Blayze had walked over to the bar and was chatting with the bartender.

"So, what do we do? Just have a look around and pick out our dinner? Like selecting a lobster at the seafood restaurant?"

"We wait. They come to us." Khalan crossed his arms over his chest and glared at Blayze.

Blayze's eyes widened, and he hurried over to the woman dressed in the schoolgirl outfit.

"I knew it. I knew you had ordered *Every Man's Fantasy.*" I shook my head.

Before Khalan could answer, Blayze hurried over to us.

"Master Khalan. The female at the bar, Lucy, is very interested in you and your date. She said she's never had a ménage before."

"Hold up." I held up my hand and took a step back. "I'm not sure what Lucy is into, but let me tell you something, Blayze with a Y, that ain't my jam." I glared hard at him.

"I meant no disrespect." He gave me a wide-eyed look and wiped the sweat off his forehead. Just looking at him made me want to take a cold bath.

"I don't want the schoolgirl. She's not my type." Khalan looked around the room. He locked gazes with a guy in the corner wearing a green cape and drinking a beer. "What about him?"

Blayze followed Khalan's gaze. "John?" He looked back at Khalan. "But he's just so…normal."

"I like normal." I lifted my head.

"But Master Khalan, Lucy is willing to pay extra for…the experience." Blayze's top lip shone, and I could smell the sweat coming off him. Those leather pants were going to be really funky by the time this night was over.

"I said we will take John," Khalan growled.

Blayze took a step back, and his eyes widened in fear. He

nodded and hurried back over to the bar, his leather pants squeaking with each step.

Khalan had turned his attention to a couple in the corner who were making out. I looked back at Blayze. He was talking to the woman who had requested Khalan. I couldn't see her face, but from the way she slammed her martini glass down on the bar, she wasn't happy.

"You make these people pay for drinking their blood?" I looked over at Khalan.

"I don't make them pay for shit. Bill is the one taking their money. I just take their blood." Khalan shrugged.

"But doesn't it seem wrong for him to profit off you?" I rubbed my temple. The slow build of a headache was brewing, and I knew if I didn't get blood soon, it would morph into a migraine.

"I am in it for the blood. What do I care if Bill makes money on the side? Besides, I can just glamour him into giving me all the profits if I want."

"And yet, I get the feeling you don't." I crossed my arms and studied him. He was an enigma to me. A monster with a heart.

"Master Khalan and R.K." Blayze stood in front of us with John at his side. "John is more than eager to please you both." Blayze nodded from the waist and backed away from us.

"Perfect," Khalan gruffed. "Let's go to the lounge."

CHAPTER 10

J followed Khalan into another part of the building. This room was off the bar area and had rounded booths with a table in the middle.

"It is my pleasure to serve my Master and his consort tonight," John said reverently.

Khalan let out a laugh that made John's eyes widen.

I jerked my head to the human and glared. "I'm not his consort."

"Slide in." Khalan motioned to me.

I started to mouth off, but his amusement quickly faded from his face. Besides, I was hungry, too. I sighed and slid into the red booth. John followed and slid in next to me. He struggled a little when his cape got caught on the end of the table. His eyes grew wide as the material tightened around his neck.

"Oh, damn. Wait. Let me help." I finally freed him from himself. Khalan stood there and rolled his eyes.

"Thanks." John's face grew red with embarrassment.

I felt bad for the guy. He was trying to play the role and ended up looking like a fool.

Khalan slid in next to him. He wasted no time and glared at the guy. The guy's eyes widened in fear as he stared back at Khalan.

"Take my blood so thou thirst may be quenched." John dramatically lowered his hood on his cape.

"You will give us your blood willingly and not remember anything after we leave. You won't remember our faces or our names. Understand?"

"Yes, Master. I understand."

"Do you really make him call you *Master*?" I crossed my arms over my chest, pretty peeved at the whole situation. I shook my head. "And what's up with all this incense. It's wreaking havoc on my sinuses."

"I'm not making him call me Master. It's his idea. And the incense keeps out werewolves." Khalan gave me a droll look before staring at John.

"You mean like Jack?"

"Listen to me, you stay away from Jack. He's trouble."

"But you had no problems taking those pups to his Pack. You must not think he's that much trouble if you left those motherless coyotes with him."

"That's not his Pack. Jack doesn't have a Pack. He's just passing through Mississippi. Besides, our kind doesn't mix with their kind." Khalan shot me a warning look.

"That's such outdated thinking." I glared.

"Expose your neck," Khalan growled at John, clearly finished with the conversation.

John obeyed and leaned his head back against the booth.

Khalan looked at me. "You remember what to do, right?"

His eyes darkened, and my stomach warmed at the way he looked at me. Something predatory and lustful hid behind his eyes, illuminated by the candlelight on the table.

"I know." My voice deepened. I swallowed, trying to regain some sense of control.

Was it the bloodlust? Was it the environment? Or was it just being with Khalan?

All of those reasons scared me, some more than others.

Khalan nodded, giving me the sign to draw first blood. I pressed my mouth to John's throat and bit down on the pulsing vein just beneath the skin.

Coppery, warm blood filled my mouth, and I moaned. I sucked hard, savoring each pull of blood.

Khalan groaned, and I opened my eyes. He wasn't drinking. He was staring at me with eyes so dark it made me want to leap over John and straddle my Maker.

Khalan finally bent his head and bit the other side of John's neck.

We were so close, I could feel Khalan's hair brush against mine. My heart rate sped up. He reached his hand up to my neck and rested his fingers against my skin. The intimate gesture had me thinking such inappropriate thoughts about Khalan that it scared me. I couldn't control my body anymore.

Another example of yet another man who was trying to control my life.

"Stop." Khalan's voice was near my ear, his breath hot on my cheek.

I pulled back from John and looked at Khalan with heavy-lidded eyes. His eyes darted to my mouth, and he groaned.

"What? Do I have blood on my lips?" I reached up to wipe them, but he caught my hand.

Everything happened so fast, it was a blur.

He slammed his mouth down across mine and kissed me hard. Lust shot through me like a red-hot arrow, and I fisted my hands in his hair to keep his mouth on mine.

He wrapped his large hands around my waist and pulled me across John's lap until I straddled him. He fisted his hands in my hair, and I ground down on his erection.

I didn't care that we were visible to all the other people in the room. All I cared about was getting my lust sated.

"How much? For the female?"

Khalan pulled his mouth from me, and I groaned. I didn't want to stop kissing him. I wanted to do other things with him.

"What did you say?" Khalan growled at the man wearing a kilt.

"How much for the female?" He trained his eyes on me and looked me up and down. I cringed.

"You're really not my type," I snarked. "I don't date guys that wear skirts."

"I don't want to date. I just want to fuck," Mr. Kilt stated.

Khalan roared like a beast. He pulled me off him and jumped up from the booth. He grabbed the guy by the collar of his tunic and lifted him into the air. "She's not yours. She's mine. And if you ever approach her again, I will rip your throat out."

"Master Khalan." Blayze hurried over to the action. He pleaded with Khalan while trying to get him to let go of the guy in the kilt. "He's new. He doesn't know the rules here. I promise I won't ever let him in again."

"You better not." Khalan shot Blayze a warning look and let go of the kilted asshole. Mr. Kilt fell to the ground in a heap.

Khalan grabbed my hand and hurried me out of the building. Once outside, I stopped and tried to catch my breath.

"Does that normally happen?" I looked at him from under my lashes.

"No. I've never had a human approach me with such disrespect." Khalan curled his hands into fists and lifted his face to the night sky.

"I meant, have you ever brought another female to this

55

club and, after drinking from a human, started making out with her in front of everyone?" I swallowed and forced myself to look at him.

He stared at me for a moment. "It's the bloodlust."

That didn't answer my question. I wanted a straight answer. Something he was never good at giving me.

CHAPTER 11

J stood there waiting for an answer I knew I wouldn't get when motion from the corner of my eye caught my attention. I wiped the taste of Khalan off my mouth with my fingertips and looked left.

Nikki.

Anger surged in my veins. I growled.

"What the fuck is she doing out here so late?" I walked over to the chain-link fence and curled my fingers into the metal as I tracked her movements.

Nikki headed from the parking lot to the building where Uncle Stan had his private investigation agency. There were no other businesses open this late except for his.

I blinked.

"What are you doing?" Khalan asked from behind me. His breath touched my hair, sending a little shiver of pleasure through me. I tried to ignore the excitement he made me feel when he was so close. It was scary to think that I was having such a physical reaction to a guy. Especially an undead one.

I swallowed hard. "I'm watching my ex-BFF. Why is she going to Uncle Stan's office?"

"Who is Uncle Stan?" Khalan asked.

"My new employer." I shrugged.

"Ah. Yes. So, you really want to get a job to support your-self instead of making your ex-husband pay where it counts?" He chuckled. "Funny, I would have figured you wouldn't let him manipulate you anymore."

"I'm not letting him manipulate me." I narrowed my eyes.

"He probably gave you some sob story about how he got his flashy mid-life crisis car repo'd. And how he's living above Mrs. Grishom's garage."

I turned and looked at Khalan. "If you already knew all that, why did you ask?" I turned back to the building. "Besides, I'm not getting a job for him. I'm working because of my daughters. They don't even want to see him anymore because he's depressed and living in a roach motel.

I can't depend on that money forever. I need to be more independent." I shrugged.

The light in Stan's office came on.

"Come on." I leapt over the chain-link fence and landed on the other side. With fresh blood in my system, I felt like I could take on anything. Even my ex-best friend who had betrayed me by having an affair with my now ex-husband.

I didn't wait to see if Khalan was following me. I hoped he would at least stay so he could give me a lift home. I didn't really want to walk the twenty miles back to my house.

I stopped at the door that Nikki had entered through and turned the knob. It was still unlocked. I crept inside and headed for the staircase instead of using the elevator.

I hurried up the steps, each one creaking loudly under my feet. When I reached the right floor, I peered out into the hallway to make sure it was empty before stepping out.

A small light was on inside Uncle Stan's office. I heard muffled voices.

I crept closer and held my breath.

"I want to hire you to find my husband," Nikki said. Her voice sounded…off to me.

"I understand that your husband Brad left a suicide note and took his truck with him," Uncle Stan stated.

"Yes."

"Mrs. Stollings, I'm going to be very blunt." Uncle Stan sighed.

"Go ahead."

"Do you have any reason to believe that he's not dead? That maybe he just ran off and started a new life? It's not a secret that you were having an affair with Rachel Jones's husband, Miles. Some men can't handle the humiliation and want to start over where no one knows their name or history."

I grinned. I liked Uncle Stan more and more with each passing minute.

"Brad wouldn't run off and leave me," Nikki said quietly. "He knew about the affair for a while. It wasn't until Rachel exposed it that Brad realized our marriage was truly over. It devastated him."

"I see. So now you want me to find him because…?"

"Well, the life insurance won't pay out until I have some kind of confirmation of his death."

"Bitch," I whispered to myself. A hand came from behind me and covered my mouth. I would have screamed, but I realized it was Khalan.

"So you want the life insurance money?" Uncle Stan said.

"I'm having a hard time paying the house note without Brad. I never thought I would be in this situation." Her voice quavered.

"There, there, Mrs. Stollings," Uncle Stan said softly. "I understand your position. But I do need to know how you plan on paying my fees if I take the job. Since you said yourself, you are having financial issues."

"I have a little in a savings account that Brad didn't know about. I'd been socking away a little bit every paycheck. And I can pay more after I get the payout from the life insurance. Will you take the case?"

"I will." I heard him opening a drawer. "I just need some information on your husband and a contact number to keep in touch with you."

I pulled Khalan's hand away and motioned for him to follow me back down the stairwell. At the bottom, we hurried outside and back to his bike under cover of the street's shadows.

"What are we going to do?" I looked at Khalan as he straddled the motorcycle.

"We are going home." He shrugged.

I touched his shoulder. "This is serious. They are starting an investigation to find Brad's body."

"Well, I guess they won't find it unless they are smart enough to look at the bottom of the Mississippi River." He started the engine. I climbed on behind him.

Worry edged its jagged way into my mind and reached down into my gut.

"I don't like it. What if they find him?" I tightened my arms around Khalan's waist.

"I doubt they will, but if they do, they will just assume that he was eaten alive by the catfish."

He pulled away from the street and headed back to my house.

CHAPTER 12

"*I'm the Temptress from Memphis. No one compares to me. I'm your true love and soul mate. The one you'll love in eternity.*"

I glanced in the rearview mirror at my girls in the back seat. They were both belting out country singer Memphis's newest song. Memphis was the latest country-pop star to take the records charts by storm. She was in her mid-twenties and bore a striking resemblance to Britney Spears. Her most recent hit, *Memphis Temptress,* was number one on the record charts.

She also claimed to be related to the late Elvis Presley and wore sparkly pink pantsuits that showed every curve of her perfect body.

I turned the radio down.

"Mom! Turn it back up!" Arianna's voice rose.

I sighed and complied.

"I thought you liked Memphis," Gabby said from the back seat.

"I do. I just don't like this song. Something about it rubs me the wrong way." I put my blinker on and turned into our

gated subdivision. By the time we had turned into our driveway, the song was over.

The girls scrambled out of the Volvo before I even had
my seat belt unfastened.

"Don't eat a lot of junk before dinner," I called out to
them. "I'm making lasagna tonight."

They both murmured something before disappearing
into the house.

I shut the garage door and walked inside the kitchen.

Sitting on the counter was a familiar cooler. I narrowed
my eyes.

Khalan.

I appreciated him leaving me blood before he headed out
of town, but I did not like him coming into my house when I
wasn't there. It was intrusive. Not to mention, it was sitting
out in the open. What if Arianna or Gabby had opened it?
How was I going to explain a cooler full of blood?

I sighed. If he had left me blood, that meant he was off on
some trip.

Was he at the beach? Or did he prefer someplace darker,
like Iceland?

I set down my purse on the kitchen island and pulled out
some frozen ground beef from the freezer. I gathered the
other ingredients for dinner out of the pantry just as my
phone trilled.

I answered it on the third ring.

"Hello?"

"Rachel. Don't hang up. It's Nikki."

My heart thumped loudly in my chest. Something came
over me, and I froze, unable to speak or hang up.

"Rachel? Are you there?" Nikki's voice was soft. But I
wasn't fooled. She was a viper who'd hidden her true self for
years. She was someone I had trusted with my heart and my
family. And she'd betrayed me.

"I'm here." My voice was eerily calm.

"I know this is awkward, but I need to talk to you. It's about Brad."

I felt my face heat with anger. No *"sorry I slept with your husband"* or *"sorry I betrayed you and wrecked your marriage."* Once again, Nikki made it all about her.

"Why are you so concerned with your husband now, Nikki?" I tightened my hold on the phone. "It seems if you had paid more attention to your man instead of mine, you wouldn't be in this predicament."

"Rachel, I know that you're angry. And you are entitled to your feelings. But I'm trying to find out where Brad is."

"Nikki, you are the most selfish bitch I have ever met in my life. It's all over town that Brad left a suicide note and took off in his truck. That leaves only one option as to where he is."

"Did he talk to you? About anything?" she asked carefully.

Unease snaked down my spine. Why was she asking me these questions now? Had someone seen me get into the truck with Brad on the last night he had been seen alive?

"The only thing Brad ever talked to me about was you. He talked about how broken-hearted he was that you were screwing around on him."

Nikki was silent. I hoped I had hurt her with my words like she'd hurt me with her actions, but I was doubtful.

"But did he say anything else? Like if he was going out of town or anything like that?"

I pressed my lips into a thin line. "I'm done with this conversation. And I'm done with you. Never call me again. Understand?" I didn't wait for her to verify if she'd heard me or not. Instead, I hung up on her.

I looked down at my trembling hands. Was it anger? Was it fear? I needed to talk to Khalan and tell him about the conversation. But in his typical fashion, he was out of town.

JODI VAUGHN

I shook my head and took a deep breath to clear my thoughts.

I had too much on my plate to worry about this now.

I had a career to think about, and lasagna to make.

* * *

"This is good, Mom." Gabby smiled around a mouthful of pasta.

"Thank you. But remember not to speak with your mouth full." I gave her a stern look.

"She'll never make it through Cotillion." Arianna smirked. "She's already late even taking the classes."

"I don't want to go through Cotillion." Gabby frowned. "I'd rather go through sword-fighting class."

"Sorry. There are no sword-fighting classes in Mississippi." I sighed. "Just Cotillion."

"Ugh." Gabby stabbed some salad with her fork.

I had let Gabby off easy. When Arianna was younger she had taken the pre-cotillion as well as the junior cotillion classes and loved them. But when I brought up it up to Gabby she pitched a fit. Something she normally didn't do. So I didn't force her to do pre-cotillion with the clear understanding she would participate in junior cotillion. I really wasn't looking forward to that day.

Arianna stared down at her pasta and moved it around on her plate.

"What's wrong, honey? Do you not like it?"

"It's fine." She didn't look up from her food.

"She's just mad 'cause her friends got to do amazing vacations this summer. And we didn't because of the divorce," Gabby said.

Arianna shot her a warning glare. I knew from that look that Gabby had hit the nail on the head.

"I know you girls are used to going on vacations every year." I cleared my throat. "I guess we are living a new normal, and it's taking some getting used to."

"It's okay. I know we don't have the money for stuff like that." Arianna shrugged.

My heart sank. The fact was that we *did* have the money. The issue was me being a vampire. Going to the beach for a week literally made me feel nauseous. But I knew I had to find a way around this situation.

"Since we didn't do a vacation this summer, maybe we could do something else. Something special." I looked between them both.

Arianna jerked her head up from her plate and looked at me with hope in her eyes. "Really?"

"Of course." I smiled. "We'll just have to look on the internet to get some ideas."

"Well, there is this one small thing that is coming up." Arianna looked over at Gabby. Gabby stopped eating and dropped her fork. "And it's something we would both like."

"Yes, Mommy, please say yes." Gabby jumped in her seat.

I laughed at her unbridled enthusiasm. Whatever this special thing was, I was going to try and make it happen.

"What is it?"

"There's a concert. In Memphis," Arianna said hopefully. "And it's on a Saturday night."

"Who is it? I'll have to see how hard it is to get tickets." I took a drink of my wine.

"Memphis."

"You already told me it's in Memphis. But who's the singer?"

"That's who it is. Memphis."

"You mean that country singer that claims to be related to Elvis Presley?" I cocked my head.

"Yes!" Arianna's face was lit up like a Christmas tree. I had not seen her look this happy in a while. I knew I had to make this happen.

"Let me find out how much the tickets are, and I'll see what I can do." I hoped the concert was at night and not some all-day event. I hoped even more that there were tickets available. Memphis was very popular, and I knew it would be hard to get seats.

"You promise?" Arianna cocked her head at me and narrowed her assessing gaze. "I mean, you're not just saying this to appease us and then tell us the tickets are all sold out? I know you don't like her all that much."

"I never said I didn't like her. Like I said earlier, I just don't like her latest song." I shrugged. "The other songs are fine."

"I understand if you can't get tickets." Arianna's voice grew soft, and she looked away. "I know things are different now."

My throat tightened. I hated to see my daughter like this. If it was the last thing I did, I was getting those damn tickets.

"I'll get them." I lifted my chin, and Arianna looked at me. Her eyes shone with unspoken hope.

"You will?"

I narrowed my gaze. "I will do my best. I just have to make sure there are tickets left."

I watched as a hopeful smile played on her innocent lips. She nodded and went back to eating her dinner.

As soon as the meal was over, I was going to grab my laptop and power it up. I needed to find those damn tickets and fast.

CHAPTER 13

I found the listing for the Memphis in Memphis concert. I could not believe how much they were asking for an outdoor show—over three hundred dollars a ticket, *and* you had to bring your own chairs.

I pulled out my credit card and ordered three without blinking. I was grateful that the concert started at nine at night. That would be when I was at my peak and could make it through the whole thing without falling asleep.

After I bought the tickets, my phone rang.

"Hello?"

"Rachel? It's Stan."

"Hey, Stan." I sat up straight. "What's up?"

"We have a new development on our client."

"The one who is trying to trap her husband in an affair?" I tried to keep the judgement out of my voice, but I didn't think I nailed it.

"That's the one. It seems like the husband is going to be in Memphis next weekend. So, we are setting up the entrapment there instead of in Charming. It actually works out

67

better since he's more likely to take the bait out of town." Stan chuckled.

"Next weekend?" I glanced down at the date of the Memphis in Memphis concert. My heart sank. It was the same date.

"Yeah. Do you have plans? 'Cause if you do, I can always hire the next photographer. He's been calling every day to see if I have a position available."

Shit. I needed the job. It was something I was actually good at. But I also needed to take my girls to the concert. Unwittingly, I found myself in a conundrum.

"What time is the entrapment supposed to start?" I asked.

"The husband is supposed to arrive at the hotel around six. He's known for visiting the bar, according to his wife, so he'll probably grab a drink around seven. We should have our girl down there at that time."

I nodded. I could snap the pictures and still have time to take my girls to the concert.

"That won't be a problem. I would like to get to the hotel a few hours early so I can get settled in and meet the bait girl so I know I have the right person."

"Ha, ha. Bait girl. I like that term. I'll have to start using it." Uncle Stan laughed. "He's staying at the Peabody. Come by the office, and I'll give you a packet with his information and a picture. I'll put you up in the hotel and give you the confirmation number."

"What kind of room are you giving me?" I debated telling him that I was taking my girls to the concert. I decided against it. I didn't want him to know how I had to juggle my life to accommodate my work schedule. I needed this job.

"I'm putting you up in the Presidential Suite at the Peabody. The room is charged on my card, and you can order room service when you want to eat. I pay for my employees' travel and food."

"Thank you." I mentally remembered how big the Presidential Suite was at the famous hotel. Miles had taken me there on our anniversary a few years ago. It would be plenty big for me and the girls plus someone else.

"I need good pictures of the husband, Rachel. My client is paying big bucks for this, and that means big bucks for you." Uncle Stan lowered his voice.

"I don't understand why she wants a divorce this badly. I get the whole the church kicking her out thing, but..."

"It goes deeper than that. She wants a divorce because he's abusing her. The church has turned a blind eye to it. But if she has pictures of infidelity, they won't turn a blind eye to *that*. They'll kick him out and grant her a divorce while letting her stay in the fellowship."

My gut turned. "I don't think I would want to associate with people like that. I imagine I would divorce the bastard and tell the congregation to kiss my ass."

"That's where you are different, Rachel. Some women aren't that strong. You don't mind standing up for what is right and damn the consequences. A lot of women aren't like you. That's why I am here, doing what I do."

His words struck a chord in me. "I don't think I'm strong." A lot of times, I felt as weak as a kitten.

"Oh, you are. Years from now, when your girls are grown, they will tell you how much of an influence you were on their lives. They'll thank you for standing up to their father. Even though it hurt them at the time."

Silence stretched between us as I soaked in Stan's words.

"But until then, I need you to get these pictures for me. And make sure they're good. There's also a bonus included."

"A bonus?"

"Yeah. You'll get an extra five thousand dollars on top of what you're already going to earn.

My mouth dropped. I started to speak, but Uncle Stan had beat me to it.

"I'll see you tomorrow." Uncle Stan ended the call.

I flopped back on the couch and stared up at the ceiling. Even if I got the pictures before the concert, I would have to leave the girls in the room for an hour or two to do it. I didn't like leaving my children alone, even if it was at the Peabody.

I wondered if one of the other moms was going to the concert. It was too late to call tonight and find out. I would call first thing in the morning. Maybe I could get someone to go with me and watch the girls for those few hours while I snapped some pictures.

I debated asking Khalan if he would go and just keep an eye on the room. I couldn't do that. He was already gone on some kind of vacation, and I didn't know how to contact him.

He'd probably bitch about me trying to do this job and take care of my girls. He had a way of making me feel like I was more of a burden to him than a normal progeny should be.

I put my computer away and headed toward the girls' rooms.

Arianna was fast asleep, her beautiful face looking more like an angel than a human. She had her hands pillowed together under her cheek as she breathed in slow, deep breaths.

I smiled. I hoped she was having beautiful dreams of summertime fun with her friends.

I tiptoed back to Gabby's room and peeked in. She was snuggled down deep in her covers. Her brows were knit together as she dreamed, probably of dragons and knights and sword fights.

I shook my head and closed the door behind me.

My girls were as polar opposite as they came.

I opened the French doors leading to the back yard and stepped outside. I walked over to the lounge chair and sat. I stared up at the night sky. The tiny pinpricks of stars scattered the dark expanse. I couldn't help but feel miniscule and insignificant against the trillions and trillions of lights in the sky.

I came out to stare up at the night sky so many times after I had found out about Miles' affair. I had never felt so alone as I did then, and the night sky seemed to give confirmation of how small I was.

Now, months after the fall of the betrayal and the finalization of my divorce, I had a different emotion when I looked up at the sky. It was more like gratitude. I had my girls, my home, and my life.

I'd lost my marriage, but I'd rather be alone in this world than stay with someone I knew I could never trust again.

I bit my lip. I might never get married again. Not that it mattered anyway. I was a vampire now. I would outlive any normal man, and I wasn't sure that vampires even married.

I guess I was destined to walk this life alone.

CHAPTER 14

I rolled down the window of my Volvo when I saw Stephanie Miller approach me in the car line.

"Thank you so much for asking us to share a room with you, Rachel. I wasn't sure we were going to be able to spend the night because all the nice hotels in Memphis were all booked up due to the concert." Stephanie was one of the women I went to church with. She was a devout Christian who had been sucked in by Veronica's fakeness and believed that the woman could do no wrong. While we were friendly, we weren't that close.

"You're welcome." I shaded my hand over my sunglasses. I didn't want to tell her that she had been my last option. All the other moms were already sharing rooms with each other. It hurt my feelings that they hadn't thought to ask if I was taking my girls. I let my friend Gina know.

Gina said the other moms didn't ask because they knew I had not taken my girls on vacation this year. They assumed my funds were tight since I was newly divorced.

I wondered if that was the real reason. I had heard the stories that after a couple got divorced, the friends either picked sides, the husband or the wife. Maybe that was the reason. They'd chosen Miles over me.

"Are you sure you don't want to split the cost for the room? I know the Peabody is expensive." Stephanie worried her lip with her teeth.

"Nope. It's already covered." I studied her through my sunglasses. "You know, I have to admit, I didn't know if you were going to let Mary Beth go and see Memphis. I didn't know you let her listen to pop or country music." In fact, all I ever heard her listen to was Christian.

Stephanie's face turned red. She ducked her head. "I have to admit, it was a hard decision. I know I'm very strict about what I let my daughter watch and listen to. People seem to think I'm a goody two shoes."

I forced myself to keep my expression stoic. "No, they don't," I lied.

That's exactly what everyone thought. Stephanie was a good Christian mom who had Bible study in her home and volunteered with the ministry at church. She held herself to an impossible standard that no one could measure up to, and I always felt like she was judging me because I didn't volunteer enough or that I liked to drink wine.

She'd freak if she knew I was now drinking blood. Probably call me a demon or something.

"I know that's what people think, Rachel." Her voice was soft. "I'm just trying to hold onto my values while living in the world. Mary Beth loves Memphis, and she never asks for anything. This was the one concert she asked to see. I kind of figured she deserved it." Stephanie shrugged.

I smiled. "You're a good mama. Don't let anyone tell you otherwise."

Stephanie smiled and walked back to her car. In my rearview mirror, I spotted Veronica pulling into the car line.

She honked. I locked my door and made sure the window was rolled up.

I hated Veronica like I loathed Herpes.

She was a pit viper when it came to gossip. Everyone stayed away from her. But the majority of people feared her enough not to get on her bad side.

I, unfortunately, was not one of those people. I was done taking shit from assholes like her.

"Rachel!" She squawked out my name before she made it to my car. The hairs on the back of my neck stood at attention.

She knocked on the driver's side window. "Rachel, you will not guess who is going to see Memphis in Memphis." Her lips curled into an evil smile. Her eyes glinted like pieces of black coal straight from the bowels of Hell.

I pulled down my sunglasses to stare at her. She made the motion for me to roll down my window.

"Those tickets cost me two hundred dollars, but my Elizabeth Grace is worth it." She lifted her chin and sneered. "We are staying in one of the hotels downtown, as well. Making a weekend out of it."

I blinked and then rolled down the window.

"I would invite you and your girls to go, but I know money's tight for you," she mocked.

Anger boiled in my veins, and I clenched the steering wheel until my knuckles turned white. The school bell rang. I knew it was petty, but I couldn't help it. Veronica had been a boulder in my shoe for too damn long.

I smirked. "Actually, I am taking the girls to see the concert. We already have our tickets. I was going to surprise the girls today."

Veronica's smile slipped. "I guess some people use their child support payments for unnecessary things like that."

I glared. "I didn't need to. Don't get it twisted, Veronica. I have my own money. Where did you say you were staying in Memphis?"

She bristled under my question. "Everything is booked up, so we took one of the last rooms at the Sheraton."

"Really? We secured a room at the Peabody." I smirked.

Shock and outrage stretched across her evil face. "But that's impossible. I tried getting rooms, and they said they were sold out."

"I guess you should have asked for the Presidential Suite." I pressed the button and rolled up my window. I watched her face shrivel into look of hatred.

I looked back at the school entrance as the kids hurried out. Arianna and Gabby made their way over to the car and climbed in.

"Hey, girls. How was school?" I looked at them through my rearview mirror. Gabby was her happy, unconcerned self. Arianna just shrugged.

"Fine," Arianna said and pulled out her phone.

"It was awful. We had to have recess in the gym because it was too wet to go on the playground. They made us run around the gym so we could release our energy, but I got in trouble when I tried to play sword fight with the janitor's mop." Gabby frowned. "Apparently, the principal got in my way as I was swinging it and got hit in the face with a mop full of bathroom floor water."

"Gabby." My eyes grew wide.

"What?" she asked. "He should have watched where he was going. It wasn't my fault that they don't allow us to play any good games in the gym." She rolled her eyes.

Arianna grinned. "You're lucky he didn't give you detention."

"I think he was too busy running for the bathroom to wash his face. I didn't wait around for him to show back up. I went over and sat by Neely Ray, who has asthma."

"Gabby. Please tell me you apologized." I glared at my daughter in the mirror.

"I did, but I'm pretty sure he was running too fast to hear me." She shrugged and pulled a book out of her backpack. "I checked out this new sci-fi book from the library today. It has zombies and aliens."

"Sounds stupid." Arianna snorted.

"It's way cooler than those teen werewolf books you are always reading. Who wants a werewolf to kiss them? That's like getting a kiss from a sloppy dog." Gabby turned up her nose.

"It figures you'd prefer zombies over a werewolf." Arianna glared.

"All right, all right. Both of you, stop." I pulled out of the car line and onto the street. I made my way to the next red light and stopped.

"Other than hitting the principal with a dirty mop, did anything else exciting happen?"

"Yeah. I found out that all my friends are going to see Memphis in Memphis. They all have their tickets. Even Laura's mom is letting her go." Arianna crossed her arms.

"Is that so?" I asked, pressing my lips together to hold in my smile. "Well, I have some news for both of you guys."

"What? Are we having chicken spaghetti tonight?" Gabby asked with excitement.

My Gabby. Little pleasures always made her happy. The world needed more people like her..

"Maybe. I haven't thought about dinner. But that's not what I wanted to tell you." I looked at them before pulling through the green light.

"The surprise is, I have tickets for all of us to go to the Memphis in Memphis concert."

"What?!" Arianna screamed. I jumped in my seat a little. "Are you serious? Is this for real?

"Yep, totally serious and very real." It felt good to be able to surprise my girls.

Arianna's face broke out into the biggest smile I had ever seen. "I have to call my friends." She pulled out her cell phone.

"Well, before you do, there's more." I turned off the street into our subdivision.

"What? What could be better than going to the Memphis in Memphis concert?" Gabby clapped her hands. She broke out into a chorus of Memphis's latest tune.

"Well…" The singing stopped, and the car grew very quiet. I made sure that they were both giving me their full attention before I continued.

"What is it?" Arianna whined. "You're killing me, Mom!"

I grinned. "We are spending the night at the Peabody. In the Presidential Suite. With Stephanie Miller and Mary Beth."

"The Peabody!" Arianna gasped.

"Is that where the ducks live?" Gabby asked.

"Yes, honey. You get to see the ducks walk into the fountain." I grinned. I looked at Arianna and noticed her face fall.

"What's wrong, Arianna? Are you not happy about this?"

"I am. It's just I wasn't expecting to go with Mary Beth and her mom."

"Well, they wanted to share the room with us. And I thought it would be nice to ask them." I pulled into our garage and killed the engine. I turned around in my seat. "Are you mad that I asked her?"

"I just wish you would have asked one of my other friends." She shrugged. "I'm shocked that Stephanie's even letting Mary Beth go see Memphis. She never lets her do anything fun."

"I think she knows this means a lot to Mary Beth. That's why Stephanie is taking her."

Arianna nodded.

"I don't care if we have to room with a hippopotamus, I'm just glad to be going," Gabby said.

"Me, too." Arianna nodded, and a smile broke out across her face. "Plus, none of my friends are staying at the Peabody. So, there's that."

"There's that," I agreed. "I may check you girls out early so we can have some fun around Memphis before the show." We all got out of the car.

"Really?" Arianna's face lit up.

"I think you girls deserve a nice weekend. It's been a long time since we did something fun."

"Thanks, Mom." Arianna threw her arms around me and hugged me tightly. I held her close and blinked back the tears that threatened to stream down my face.

When she pulled away, she looked so happy. "I'm going to call my friends." She raced to her bedroom with her phone in her hand.

"Thanks, Mommy." Gabby gave me a tight hug. "Do you think we'll get close enough where Memphis can touch my hand?"

"I don't know, honey. It's open seating, and it's outside. We are bringing our chairs. So, if we get there early enough, we should get good seats."

She clapped her hands and headed back to her room.

I smiled to myself. Despite all the crap we'd gone through, tonight had been a breakthrough. It felt like I was finally getting my happy girls back.

CHAPTER 15

*T*he days passed slowly. The girls woke up every day excited about the upcoming Memphis in Memphis concert.

They had told Miles that we were going when he stopped by to see them one afternoon. I expected him to be a little irritated. The old Miles would have told me not to waste money on something so trivial. But since the divorce, Miles didn't seem quite like himself. Instead, he'd appeared a little sad that he hadn't been included.

Maybe now he saw that he'd lost more than a wife. He'd also lost a family.

I wondered if he and Nikki were still an item. But there was no way I was going to ask. I knew that Nikki was trying to get Brad's life insurance money and I figured part of it was because I had come out pretty good financially after the divorce.

It seemed like such a waste. Two families torn apart by two selfish individuals.

It had been a few days since I'd last had blood with

Khalan. I would need some soon, and I didn't know when he would be back.

It was Friday night, and the girls were spending the night at a friend's house. Since they had been picked up by their friend's mom after school, I didn't have to wait in the car line. Instead, I had slept the whole day and afternoon away. I woke up just as the light was fading and gave way to the night.

I sat in bed, staring at the dark shadows in my room.

For the first time in a long while, I felt at peace. I threw my legs over the side of the bed and stood. The girls would be back tomorrow morning, so if I wanted to go out and get blood, I needed to do it tonight while I was alone.

I headed to the bathroom to prepare for my night.

After getting ready, I decided to wait until later to go out and get blood. I didn't want anyone to see me, so I decided to leave around midnight. During that time, I enjoyed a glass of cabernet and watched a couple of movies. By midnight, I was anxious and ready to go out and feed. My lust for blood had begun to increase over the last few weeks, and after hunting with Khalan, I knew I could never go back to drinking anything but human blood.

Around twelve thirty, I pulled out of my garage, ready to eat.

Our subdivision was dark except for the few security lights along the ends of the streets.

I pulled out of the safety of my neighborhood and onto the street. My heart suddenly lodged in my throat as I made my way closer to downtown Charming. I had been excited when I was getting ready, but now that the time had come for me to take blood from another human, I was very nervous.

I took some slow, deep breaths as I maneuvered through

the streets of downtown. I pulled into a parking spot away from the buildings and killed the engine.

I took one last look in the mirror and grabbed my purse. I kept my head down as I walked over to the same building that Khalan had taken me to before. I passed a couple of drunk guys who made a few catcalls but didn't try to follow me. Even if they had tried something, I knew I could take them. Another plus of being a vampire was my increased strength.

I spotted the tattoo parlor ahead. The business was lit up inside, but no customers sat around waiting. I walked inside, and the receptionist didn't look up from his comic book.

"We're closed."

"I know." I lifted my chin. "I'm not here for a tattoo."

The dark-haired guy looked up when I spoke. His eyes drifted from my face down my body. "Too bad. With a body like that, it would be like painting the Mona Lisa." He grinned.

I narrowed my eyes on him and debated taking his blood. But I figured he would like it too much.

"You will forget I was ever here." I walked past him down the hall to the door that led out into the alley like Khalan had shown me.

The door slammed behind me, and I was alone in the alley. I curled my fingers into fists and took a deep breath. I walked down the lane, away from the security lights. My eyes adjusted to the darkness, and I saw a woman with blond hair standing in the shadows. She was staring at the ground so I couldn't make out her face.

She didn't speak but walked toward me with her head down.

My heart thumped in my chest. What if it was someone I knew? Could I still go through with it?

Unease burned in my chest. I needed blood. I didn't know when I'd have another night to get it without having to leave my girls alone.

I forced one foot in front of the other and met the stranger halfway.

"I'm here…"

"You're here for me," she said softly without looking up.

My heart lurched. "Maybe you're not the one I'm looking for."

Her head jerked up. Her large, brown eyes stared up at me. "Please, don't reject me. I need the money. Besides, I haven't had anything to drink…tonight. And I'm not on drugs." She blinked rapidly. "My blood is healthy. I promise."

I stepped back into the shadows. Shit. She knew what I was.

"Maybe I'm just out here looking for a…date." It was the only thing that came to mind other than drugs. And I couldn't bring myself to say I was out looking to score drugs.

"I know you're here for blood." She took another step toward me. "Blayze won't let me into the club because I have no money. This is something I've wanted to do for a while, but I'm broke."

"Blayze?" I repeated. The same guy that had arranged for a blood donor for Khalan the first night we'd come out together.

"Yes. He promised to offer me to the Master."

"So, Blayze is your pimp?" I narrowed my eyes at her. Suddenly, I had a horrible feeling about this.

She blinked and then shook her head. "What? No. I'm not here for sex. I'm here so you can take my blood."

"I used to get paid but since Blayze is in charge, now he makes us pay."

"Shit," I muttered.

"Please don't misunderstand me. I gladly offer up my

blood. I signed a waiver and everything. Blayze has my history and blood work on file. He promised me that I would be the next to be offered to the Master. If I could just come up with the money." She looked down at the ground.

I glared. "How much money does Blayze want?"

"A thousand dollars."

"Are you kidding me?" I nearly choked.

"What? Should I have paid more? Is that why I wasn't chosen?" She blinked up at me like a doe in headlights.

"Do you know what I am?" I stepped out of the shadows.

"Yes. You're part of a specialized group who roleplays fantasy characters. You are part of the Vampire Coven of Mississippi. Although I expected you to be dressed in a cape with black, thigh-high boots and not yoga pants and sneakers."

My mouth dropped. She had no idea I was a real, honest to God vampire.

I nodded. "Are you sure you want to …roleplay?"

"Yes. But I don't have any money."

"I don't want your money."

"Really?" Her eyes lit up. "I hope I please you. If you like the experience, I'm open to scheduling another session." Her eyes grew wide with hope.

"All right."

"Where do you want me? Shall we go inside the building to the bar?" She smiled brightly up at me. She clapped her hands together in excitement. "I'm sorry. I've never been sacrificed to a vampire before. I can hardly contain myself."

"What's your name?" I rubbed my temple and closed my eyes.

"Jennifer."

"First of all, Jennifer, you need to calm down a little."

"Okay. I can do that." She closed her eyes and took a deep

breath. When she opened them, she smiled up at me. "Do you want to go inside?"

"No. Let's just go over here in the corner." My voice shook. Guilt washed over me. I couldn't help but feel like I was taking this poor girl's choice away.

I took a deep breath and looked her in the eyes. "After this is done, you won't remember this night. You won't remember my face or what we did here. After this, you will go home, eat something, and go to sleep."

Her eyes glazed over, and her mouth parted. She turned her head to the side, exposing her neck to me.

I saw the vein pulsing with warm blood. My mouth watered. I swallowed and wrapped my hands around her neck and bit down on her flesh.

Warm, coppery fluid poured onto my tongue. I sighed as I sucked the life-giving elixir into my mouth. It was better than the most expensive wine I had ever tasted.

I sighed with pleasure as I drank from her. I opened my eyes and realized I needed to let her go.

A part of me really did not want to stop drinking, but I knew what could happen if I took too much blood from a person. If I lost control, I could accidentally kill them.

I pulled away and looked in Jennifer's eyes.

"Go home and go to sleep. You won't remember this night."

Jennifer nodded and trotted down the alley toward the parking lot. The door to the building burst open, and Blayze stepped out. His eyes widened when he spotted me.

"Mistress Rachel. I wasn't expecting you." Sweat popped out on his forehead, and he wiped his hand over his sweaty upper lip. His eyes darted around before falling back on me. "Can I offer you a sacrifice to quench your thirst?"

"Bill…"

"It's Blayze," he corrected.

I narrowed my eyes. "Blayze, I need to ask you something. And you better not lie to me."

His eyes widened as I took a step toward him.

"Are people paying you to...roleplay?" I wasn't sure if he actually knew that we were vampires. So I had to be careful about how I worded my question.

"Well, yes. I mean, it's a service that is needed. Masters need living sacrifices, and there are those who are more than willing."

"And how much are you giving Khalan?" I leaned into his personal space. I could smell the fear pouring off him.

He licked his trembling lips. "Well..."

"Don't lie to me, Blayze."

"I don't exactly pay Khalan."

"So, you are the only one making money off this situation?" I arched my eyebrows.

"Money's not everything. I mean, Khalan and the players both get to roleplay. That's what they really want."

"And what *you* really want is cold, hard cash," I stated.

"Well..."

"Blayze, you have one chance to tell me the truth," I warned.

He dropped his head and studied the ground. "I had been part of another roleplaying group in Alabama. It was more werewolves and Fae. When I moved to Charming, I felt alone, so I started an online roleplaying group for vampires." He looked up at me and blinked. "Everyone liked it so much, they kept asking when I was going to have a place set up for everyone to meet and roleplay in person. It wasn't until I saw Khalan out late one night that I knew I had found the guy to play my vampire. I approached him and told him about the roleplaying and said he would make a great vampire and that it would be fun.

I didn't start charging until a month into it. I had so many people who wanted the experience of being with a vampire that they started offering me money. I was working at a bookstore in Oxford at the time and not making a lot of money. Once I started charging, I couldn't believe the amount I made. So, I quit working at the bookstore and concentrated on the roleplaying. There's a monthly fee to belong. And to be chosen as a blood donor, you bid at an online auction. The winner gets to be with Master Khalan, or now, his Mistress."

"I'm not his Mistress," I growled.

"My mistake. I meant no disrespect. He seems to protect you like his consort." Blayze wiped his sweaty brow.

"Consort?"

"You know, like a spouse."

I barked out a laugh. "Yeah. I'm not that either."

"So, if people bid at an auction, what was with the girl the other night? The one who you were talking with at the bar with the school girl outfit. The one that seemed upset."

He cleared his throat and looked away. "She thought she was going with Khalan that night. She didn't know that someone else had outbid her. She wasn't happy about it."

"It sounds to me like you took her money, and when she didn't get her time with Khalan, she got pissed."

Bill jerked up his head at me. I knew I was right.

"I can't help but think you are doing this with other role players."

The color drained from his face.

"So, I'm going to give you a chance to make this right. You are going to give back money to the people who never got what they wanted. And you are going to be honest with Khalan about how much money you are charging these people."

"But."

"But, nothing. If you don't tell *the Master*, I will. And it will be a thousand times worse if I do it." I poked him in the chest and turned on my heel.

I walked down the dark alley with a smirk on my face. I might be a vampire, but at least I didn't take advantage of the weak.

CHAPTER 16

$\mathscr{I}$ packed our clothes on Thursday evening for the concert that weekend. We were leaving Friday so the girls could see some of downtown Memphis. The show was on Saturday, the same night I was being paid to get those discriminating photos. The girls were already asleep, and now it was my turn to pack my bags. I had no idea what to wear to an outdoor concert, so I decided on jeans, a T-shirt, and some sneakers.

I packed a couple of nice outfits because I had reserved a tea time at the Peabody for the girls and me. It was expensive but well worth it. I wanted to treat them to the experience of a lifetime.

When I was finished, I grabbed my bottle of wine and headed out to the back yard. Since becoming a vampire, I tended to gravitate to hanging out in my yard and staring up at the sky.

I wasn't used to alone time. When I was married, after the kids had gone to bed, Miles and I would either watch a movie with a glass of wine or sit outside and talk about our days. Mainly, *he* talked since the duties of a housewife always seemed to bore him.

I was lonely. I'd never thought in a million years that I would be divorced with two children. Now that I was a vampire, that meant I couldn't get married again. At least, I couldn't marry a human. He would age and die, and I would never grow old.

I curled up into a ball on the lounge chair. Tears slid down my cheeks.

"Why are you crying?"

Khalan's voice had me squeezing my eyes tight. I didn't need to hear his admonishing words tonight.

"I'm not crying." I sat up quickly and wiped my eyes.

"I'm not blind. I can see that you are."

"It's nothing. Just having a bad day." I turned and faced him.

He wore dark jeans and a black T-shirt. My heart jumped a little at the sight of him. It was in that moment of desperation that I knew I needed to get laid.

"You look...different." My voice was husky in my own ears.

"I always wear black." He scowled and ran a hand through his hair.

"You're not wearing your coat." I cocked my head. "I don't think I've ever seen you without it."

He narrowed his gaze on me. "I saw you inside packing. Where are you going?"

"I'm taking the girls for a weekend trip."

"Where?"

"To Memphis." I shrugged.

His gaze hardened. "This weekend?"

"Yeah. We're leaving tomorrow."

He took a step toward me and got into my space. "Listen to me. I forbid you from going to Memphis."

"Excuse me?" I arched an eyebrow. All the lusty ideas I had toward my Maker were officially gone.

"You are not allowed to go to Memphis this weekend. It's too dangerous."

"You can't forbid me from doing anything." I propped my hands on my hips and glared. This was not a pissing contest he was going to win.

"Do you know how many people are going to be in Memphis this weekend? It's too dangerous for you to be there. You'll likely be discovered as a vampire. Then you'll have the entire human race trying to come at us with stakes and holy water."

"You said holy water doesn't work."

"I said nothing about the stakes." His dark eyes glinted.

"I have to go this weekend. I have a job there."

"Tell your boss you can't make it." He turned to leave and then looked back over his shoulder. "Whatever you do, don't go to Memphis. It's too dangerous. If you get in trouble there, I can't help you."

I watched him walk out the gate of my fence and into the dark woods that bordered my house.

He acted like I was a moron. I knew how to stay out of trouble and not let anyone know that I was a vampire. I glared into the darkness. How dare he try and tell me how to live my life?

For too many years, I had let Miles make all decisions for me and run things. I was a single woman now. Khalan maybe my Maker, but he sure as hell didn't run my life.

CHAPTER 17

"*A*re you guys ready for some fun?" I climbed into the front seat of the Volvo and started the engine. I looked at my girls in the rearview mirror.

"Yes. I can't believe you checked us out of school early." Arianna grinned. "My friends are so jealous that we are going to Memphis a day early. They're not leaving until tomorrow morning."

"I wish Melanie could have gone." Gabby scowled.

"I'm sorry, honey. Maybe next time. I think you'll have fun anyway."

"I will, Mommy." She gave me a smile.

"I have a neat place for us to go while we are in Memphis."

"Where is it?" Gabby asked.

"It's the restaurant at the hotel."

"The expensive one?" Arianna's eyes widened. "But I didn't pack anything that nice."

"That's okay. I packed a nice dress for both you and your sister."

"Do I have to wear a dress?" Gabby sighed.

"Yes, honey. We are going to have tea, with real scones and clotted cream."

Her face lit up. "Like the Queen of England?"

I grinned. The phone rang, and I glanced down to see who was calling.

Miles.

I hit the Bluetooth button on my dash screen.

"Hello?"

"Hey, Rachel. It's Miles."

"Hi, Miles. You're on speaker phone, and the girls are in the car."

"Hi, Daddy," Arianna and Gabby called out.

"Hi, girls." I could hear the hesitation in his voice. "Why are you girls out of school so early?"

"Mommy is taking us to see Memphis in Memphis," Gabby said.

"Well, that's certainly nice." He cleared his throat. "Rachel, could you take me off Bluetooth for a minute?"

"Yes. Hold on, and I'll pull over to the gas station." I didn't want to set a bad example for the girls by using my cell phone while I drove. So, whenever they were in the car, I always pulled over.

"Can we grab a drink?" Arianna asked.

"Yes. Here's a twenty. You can both get a snack, too." I handed her the twenty-dollar bill and waited until they had walked into the convenience store.

"What's up, Miles?"

"You didn't tell me you were taking the girls out of school early."

"It was kind of last-minute. They really didn't get a family vacation, so I thought it would be nice. The girls both like Memphis."

"The city?"

"No, the singer. She goes by one name. Memphis. And claims to be related to Elvis." I snorted.

"I can't keep up."

"So, what did you want to talk to me about?" I kept my gaze trained on the front of the convenience store. I saw Gabby and Arianna standing where the chips were near the windows. They looked like they couldn't make up their mind what kind to get.

"Nikki said she called you."

And just like that, my stomach dropped. That confirmed they were still seeing each other.

"Yes."

"What exactly did she say?" His tone grew low.

"Didn't she tell you? Since you guys are together now, I figured you told each other everything."

"Rachel…"

"I can't imagine her telling me something that you don't already know." The harsh words felt good coming out of my mouth.

"I think I made a mistake in calling."

"I think you did, too. I want to keep things civil for the sake of the children." I lifted my chin.

"Yes, of course. That's all I ever wanted," he implored.

I tightened my grip on my phone. I wanted to tell him that's not all he wanted. He only looked out for himself, never for our family.

"I just didn't want her to upset you."

"How could she possibly upset me more?" I snorted. "I could care less that she's hired a private investigator to find Brad's body."

"She told you that?" His voice was incredulous.

My mouth dropped open. "Did you not know?"

"No. Of course, not." I could picture Miles shoving his hand through his blond hair and staring at the floor.

"It seems she needs to find his body for the life insurance."

"But she told me they didn't have life insurance. She said Brad was really in debt. All the times she asked for money…"

"You gave her money? While we were married?" I growled. Angry white spots danced before my eyes.

His silence was telling.

The girls walked out of the door, bag in hand. I wanted to scream and yell at my ex for being so selfish toward his family but so generous with his mistress. But I wouldn't do it in front of my children.

"I have to go." I hung up while Miles was stuttering and trying to get some words out of his lying mouth.

The car door opened, and both girls got into the back with a bag of cheese-flavored potato chips and a soda.

"Are you guys ready for some fun?" I put the car in reverse. "Because this weekend will be one for the books."

CHAPTER 18

*W*e were able to check in early at the Peabody. Uncle Stan had paid a lot of money for us to have the Presidential Suite, so they were very accommodating to our needs.

"I can't believe how beautiful this room is." Gabby looked out the window. "Can we go on the roof and look at the duck house?"

"Sure." I glanced at my watch. "Let me make a call downstairs to check on our tea reservations first."

The girls went over to the TV and turned it on.

"Really? We are in the nicest hotel in Memphis, and you girls want to watch TV?" I looked at both of them and shook my head.

I picked up the phone and called downstairs to confirm our reservations. After that, I put away our clothes and looked at the king size bed in the room.

"So, where are we all going to sleep?" Arianna eyed me.

"I'm guessing that Mary Beth and her mom will take the bed. I'll sleep in the pull out bed with both of you guys.

"But I don't think we're all going to fit." Arianna crossed

her arms. "Why don't you and Miss Stephanie take the bed and all the girls will sleep on the pull out."

"I'll take the floor" Gabby jumped up. "I don't mind."

"Thank you, honey." I brushed the top of her dark head with my fingers. "That's very generous of you. But I don't think that's necessary."

"There's a small kitchen in here." Arianna ducked into another room.

I followed her. It was a galley kitchen, small but suitable for us. There was a microwave, a coffeemaker, and a small refrigerator.

"When is Mary Beth coming?" Arianna asked as she scrolled through her phone.

"She's coming up tomorrow. I told her to get here early so we could eat lunch at Rendezvous down the block. They have the best ribs in the South."

"Ugh. Do we have to?" Arianna rolled her eyes "I was wanting a burger or something like that."

"Well, we'll see. Stephanie didn't confirm when she was getting here. We may have to grab something quick instead."

I looked at my phone. "The concert starts at nine tomorrow night. We could get a burger then and head over to the venue. Since it's outside, they are letting everyone bring lawn chairs. I packed ours plus a couple extra in case anyone forgot theirs."

"Look." Arianna flipped on the local Memphis news. They were reporting on the Memphis in Memphis concert. "They are saying the tickets are sold out." She looked at me. "I can't believe you got them in time."

"I know. I guess it was meant to be." I smiled. It felt good to give my girls something special.

"Now, we have time to walk around downtown for a little bit before." I grabbed my purse and room key. I opened the door, and the girls headed out into the hallway.

We strolled through the downtown shops and walking by the Orpheum. The girls commented on wanting to come back to see a play, and I mentally added that to my to-do list when I got home.

We did a little shopping, and I let the girls pick out a new shirt. By the time we arrived back at the Peabody, we were all tired. I hadn't anticipated being so wiped out since I'd just gotten blood the night before.

"Why don't we all relax before we start getting ready for tea?" I yawned behind my hand.

The girls both collapsed on one bed while I drew the curtains and laid down on the other. I reached for my phone on the nightstand and set the alarm so I wouldn't oversleep.

What seemed like seconds later, I was prying my eyes open at the persistent alarm. I sat up in bed and blinked.

"We thought you would oversleep and we'd get to order room service." Gabby glared.

"No such luck." I stifled a yawn. I picked up the phone and silenced the alarm. "Where's Arianna?"

"In the bathroom putting on her fancy dress." Gabby sighed. "Are you sure I can't wear what I have on?"

"No, honey. This is a very nice restaurant. Like where kings and queens dine." Her eyes widened at the reference.

"Really?"

"Yes, really. So, tonight, I need you to look like a princess."

"Maybe they will serve dragon." She made a slashing motion with her hand like she was sword fighting.

"Maybe." I laughed. I knocked on the bathroom door. "Arianna?"

"Just a minute."

The door opened, and she stepped out in a pretty, pale green dress. She had kitten heels on and had brushed her hair until it shone light black silk.

"You look beautiful, honey. Want me to put your hair up?"

97

"Sure, just don't make me look like a little girl."

"I couldn't make you look like a little girl if I tried. You look like a twenty-year-old," I huffed.

"Really?" She smiled.

"Yes." I grabbed the brush and some bobby pins. I turned the curling iron on. I fiddled and worked her hair until it was in a pretty up-do.

"I'm wearing my diamond studs that Dad got me for Christmas." She smiled in the mirror and turned her head from side to side.

I bit my lip to keep from telling her that I was the one who had searched for and bought the gift. I'd put both of our names on the tag. Somehow, she'd forgotten that.

I forced a smile and looked at her.

"You look beautiful. Now, tell your sister to come in here and let me fix her hair."

"It will take you all night to make her look pretty." Arianna snorted.

"Arianna. That's not a nice thing to say about your sister. You are both beautiful."

Gabby rounded the corner and entered the bathroom. "I'd rather have mad sword-fighting skills than be beautiful." She sighed. "Then I could slay any monster that tried to come in our house."

"Yeah. Like that weird gardener." Arianna snorted and walked out of the bathroom so Gabby could get ready.

"He's not a gardener. He's a wizard." Gabby crossed her arms. "Besides, I like him." She looked up at me. "Don't you like him, too, Mommy?"

I swallowed. "Sure. I like him all right."

"Just all right? He did carry you in the house and into the bedroom when you fainted that time. I would think you would like him a little more than all right." Gabby looked at me carefully.

My eyes widened. I had thought Khalan had glamoured her into forgetting about that incident. I had been so starved for blood that I fainted. Khalan had been there and carried me inside to my bedroom where I started drinking his blood. When the girls knocked on the door, he had disappeared out my window.

"You remember that?"

"Yeah. Khalan said you fainted because you hadn't eaten in a while. He said eating was very important, and if we miss a meal, we might faint." She frowned. "But I've forgotten to eat meals before when I was outside playing, and I don't ever remember fainting." She looked up at me.

"That's because you're so young and resilient. Besides, I think I fainted because my body was stressed out."

"Because Daddy was sneaking around with Nikki." Gabby nodded. "That's understandable."

"Gabby, I don't think I should be talking to you about this." I ran the brush through her long, dark hair.

"Fine." She stared at me in the mirror. "Do I have to wear that pink dress you brought for me?"

"Yes."

"Ugh. I don't like pink. Why can't I wear black? Or silver? Or a suit of armor? I bet kings wore suits of armor for meals. They were always almost getting killed, so they had to wear armor to dinner. You know, to protect themselves."

I laughed in spite of myself. "I'm sure you're right. But it just so happens, I don't have a suit of armor anywhere in my suitcase. So, you are just going to have to wear the pink dress."

By the time we made it downstairs, we were only five minutes early for our reservations.

I stepped up to the maître d' and smiled. "I have a reservation for tea for three under Jones."

"Ah, yes. Welcome, Mrs. Jones. If you will follow me this

way." The maître d' effortlessly weaved his way through the beautiful restaurant until he stopped at a table in the middle of the room.

He pulled out my chair, and I sat. He placed my napkin in my lap. Then he pulled out Arianna's chair and then Gabby's.

"Your waiter is Charles, and he will be with you in a minute." The man smiled, gave a small bow, and disappeared out to his post.

Gabby giggled.

"Stop being such a child." Arianna positioned her napkin in her lap.

"I can't help it. I am a child." Gabby rolled her eyes. She looked at me and grinned. "I've never had a waiter hold a chair for me."

"I told you, this is a very nice restaurant." I winked and glanced around the place, noting how almost every table was taken. I had been lucky to get reservations.

"This is going to be a real treat, girls."

"I've never been to anything like this." Arianna's wondrous tone had me smiling. I had done something right and set up something they would remember forever.

"Here is the selection of tea you ordered, ma'am. And your savory sandwiches as well as desserts." The waiter placed a tower of food on the table. "May I pour?" He held the silver teapot in his hand and awaited my command.

"Yes, please." I watched as he poured the caramel-colored tea into first my cup, then Arianna's, and lastly Gabby's.

"If you need anything else, please let me know." He gave a quick bow and left us to our delicacies.

"I don't know what to choose." Arianna grinned.

"Well first, taste your tea. It's an Oolong that I thought you would both love. You can add milk or sugar if you'd like." I pointed to the small silver pitcher of milk and the silver container of sugar.

"Look. The sugar is shaped like flowers." Gabby picked up a blue cube pressed into the shape of a daisy. She held it with the tongs until she plopped it into her china teacup.

"I think I'll just have milk." Arianna poured a bit into her tea and stirred gently. She took a sip.

"How is it?"

"It's good. But I may add a little sugar." She put a small blue daisy-shaped sugar cube into her cup and began to stir.

I preferred nothing in my tea, so I just watched the girls as they chose different sandwiches and sweets for their plates.

"Mommy, you should try this sandwich. It's so sweet," Gabby spoke.

"Don't speak with your mouth full." I shook my head. "That is a cucumber sandwich. It has cream cheese."

"Can you make these at home?" Arianna asked.

"Sure. The sandwiches and tea I can do. I'll have to look up a recipe for scones and the clotted cream."

"Clotted cream?" Arianna wrinkled her nose.

"This is clotted cream. And it tastes a lot better than it sounds. You'll like it. I promise." I pointed to the little pot of white spreadable.

I chose a sandwich and an orange-colored macaron. I bit into the tiny sandwich.

"Oh my God!" Arianna stiffened in her seat.

"What?" I looked at her and her plate. "What's wrong?" I reached for her arm.

"She's here." Arianna's eyes grew wide. I followed her gaze to the other side of the room.

"Who?" I frowned and looked around the crowded space. Had Veronica wormed her way into the Chez Pérez?

"Don't look." Arianna jerked her head from whoever she was looking at and turned to me. "She's looking at us."

"Arianna. Who is looking at us? You're not making any sense."

"It's her. It's Memphis." Arianna's face broke into a wide smile.

"The singer?" I frowned and then looked back across the room. I immediately met the gaze of a beautiful, blond woman. I recognized her from the pictures on the internet.

"Stop staring at her!" Arianna pleaded. "She's going to think we're stalking her."

"Stalking her? I have reservations. The only thing I'm stalking is this orange macaron." I huffed and took a bite of the sweet treat.

"I want to see." Gabby stood up and stared across the room.

"Gabby!" Arianna grabbed her arm to force her to sit down, but Gabby snatched her arm away. "Mom, make her chill."

"Gabby, sit down and enjoy your tea," I chided.

"Do you think she'll give me an autograph?" Gabby sat but continued craning her neck to see.

"I don't know, honey. I think she just wants to be left alone to enjoy her tea." I took a sip of my Oolong. "Both of you, stop staring and eat something. This tea cost a lot of money, and I want you to enjoy it."

"I can't believe you're not freaking out." Arianna glared at me.

"I'm saving my freaking out for tomorrow at the concert."

"I think she's coming over here," Gabby said.

"What?" Arianna turned her head. She looked back at me. "She is coming over here. Act natural."

"I am acting natural. I'm over here sipping my tea." I shrugged. "She's probably just leaving."

"But I wanted an autograph," Gabby pouted.

Arianna gasped just as Memphis stepped up to the table. I

put down my teacup to issue the singer an apology for my girls' behavior in staring at her.

"Excuse me, I'm ..."

"I know who you are. You're Memphis." I smiled. "My girls are very excited to see you in concert tomorrow night."

She blinked, and her smile widened." These are your precious girls? How wonderful." She looked from me to Arianna and then Gabby. "They are beautiful."

Arianna looked like she had died and gone to Heaven, and Gabby lifted her chin and grinned.

"Thank you so much. This is Arianna, and this is Gabby."

"Hello, Gabby." Memphis held out her hand, and Gabby took it. "Very nice to meet you."

"It's nice to meet you, too. Can I have an autograph?" Gabby said quickly.

"Gabby," I warned.

"Oh, it's okay. I don't mind one little bit." Memphis grabbed the paper menu and pulled a pen out of her clutch. She scribbled her name down and handed it back to Gabby.

"Thank you so much. I'm going to show all my friends when I get to school on Monday."

"And your name is Arianna?" Memphis turned her attention to my eldest. "What a beautiful name to go with a beautiful girl." She held out her hand.

Arianna blinked and took the singer's hand. "Thank you," she muttered. "I like your name, too."

Memphis let out a laugh. "Well, when you have the King of Rock and Roll's blood in you, you naturally have to have a Southern-sounding name."

"I can't argue with that." I laughed. "We arrived a day early so we could see a little of the city before the big day tomorrow."

"And what's your name?" She eyed me.

"Oh, I'm so sorry. How rude of me. My name is Rachel. Rachel Jones."

She cocked her head and held out her hand to me. "Nice to meet you, Rachel."

"Nice to meet you, as well." I touched her hand and was surprised to see how firm a handshake she had. She was strong for such a little woman.

"Are you enjoying your tea?" She looked back at the girls.

"Yes," they both said in unison and took a sip.

"I know you must be very busy. I'm so sorry to take up so much of your time." I felt a little awkward that she was still standing while we were all sitting.

"Not at all. I always love meeting fans. If you don't mind, I would love to join you." She whispered something to her bodyguard, and he rushed off to grab another seat.

"Of course, not. We would be honored," I said. I moved my chair down so she could sit near Arianna.

"Thank you so much." She gave us a beautiful smile. Immediately, the bodyguard placed a chair at the table.

Memphis gracefully eased into the seat and then glanced at the girls before looking back at me.

"So, are you from the Memphis area, Rachel?"

"No. we're from a small town that you've probably never heard of." I laughed.

"Oh, I bet I have. I've traveled everywhere, and I know just about every city as well as small towns." She smiled.

"We're from Charming, Miss—"

"Mississippi." She finished my sentence. Her smile slipped.

"Yes. Have you ever been there?"

"No. But I used to live in a small town in England. It was a community, really." She sighed. "And the town was called Rye. I was young and in love, and I thought I would live there forever." She shrugged.

"I didn't know you had a boyfriend." Arianna leaned forward.

"Oh, I don't. Not anymore. You see, he broke my heart and left me alone. In the dark...of my heart." She sighed melodramatically.

I blinked. I guessed singers had to be actors, as well.

"I'm sorry to hear that. But you are young, and you have plenty of time to find your soul mate." I patted her hand.

She took my hand between hers and stared into my eyes. "I hope you're right. I really do."

I pressed my lips together. She seemed like a lost child. She had everything: beauty, wealth, fame. Surely, she could get the guy, too.

"How long have you been married?" She looked at me with hopeful eyes.

"Actually, I'm divorced." I glanced at the girls. They were still in shock that Memphis was sitting at our table.

"I'm sorry. I didn't mean to pry." She pulled her hands from mine and looked down, seeming a little embarrassed at her line of questioning.

"It's okay." I nodded. "We both love the girls and are doing a pretty good job co-parenting."

She nodded then cut her eyes at me. "So, there's no one special in your life? No one you are dating?"

"Me?" I laughed. "No. I don't think I have the time to date, plus I'm happy with just raising my girls."

"Of course, you are. You are a wonderful mother." She looked at Arianna and Gabby. "You girls are lucky. You know, I lost my mom when I was very young."

"That must have been hard on you," I said sympathetically.

"It was. But that's life. You live and learn and keep plodding on. No matter what." She looked back at me. "Besides, I wouldn't worry if I were you. You are stunning, and you'll have the guys lining up around your house." She laughed.

"I doubt that." I snorted. "But thanks for the compliment."

"The only guy she has coming around the house is that scary-looking gardener," Arianna pointed out.

Memphis looked at Arianna and frowned. "Gardener?"

"Yes. Except I haven't actually seen him do any work. He's weird. We go to bed and wake up in the morning, and the flowers are planted." Arianna stared at her idol.

"Really? So, he's kind of a night owl." She grinned.

"I don't think he's actually a gardener." Gabby took a bite of her cookie. "I think he's a wizard."

"Really, a wizard? How interesting." Memphis leaned forward in her seat. "What makes you think that?"

"Gabby," I warned and then turned to Memphis. "She has a big imagination."

"That's great. I have a big imagination, as well." She smiled and looked back at Gabby. "Tell me, Gabby, why do you think he's a wizard? Can he do spells?"

"I'm not sure. He does wear this long, black coat with a hood." She shrugged and licked the icing off her cookie. "And he's got those eyes. The kind that knows things. Magic things."

I looked from my daughter to the superstar again. "I'm sorry. He's just a friend. And I'm afraid he's no magician." I took a sip of tea and glared at Gabby.

"Does this wizard like your Mommy, Gabby?" Memphis giggled.

"I think so. I mean, he carried her inside to the bed." She shrugged.

I groaned. "It's not what it sounds like. I fainted, and he just happened to be there. He carried me to the bed so I could lie down."

Memphis's smile was gone, and she shifted in her seat. She looked at the girls and then back at me.

"So, you must be excited for the concert tomorrow." I shoved a cucumber sandwich into my mouth as I felt my face go beet-red with embarrassment. She probably thought I was an unfit mother.

She brightened. "Yes, I am. I have to get there early for rehearsal. What time are you getting there?"

"Well, the tickets say we can't get in until seven. I'm sure there will be a line at the gate and a rush to get set up at the front row. It doesn't start till nine, right?"

"Yes. But I wouldn't worry about fighting the crowds. I'll put all your names on the list so you can get there before the show, and I'll have a section reserved for you in the front row."

"Really?" Arianna put her hand over her mouth.

"Yes, really." Memphis squeezed her hand and beamed.

"Thank you so much. My friends are not going to believe we are getting front-row seats."

"Wow. Thanks so much. But there's a problem." I set my teacup back in the saucer.

"Problem?" Memphis's eyes widened.

"Well, Memphis, we're sharing our room with another mom and her daughter, who don't arrive until tomorrow night. They are supposed to go to the concert with us."

"That's no problem at all. I'll add them to my list, too," Memphis said brightly. She looked at my girls. "In fact, why don't you let Gabby and Arianna come a little early. They can watch me practice, and I can show them around backstage and on the tour bus. That way, you can wait on your friend and come when she does."

I shifted in my seat. "I don't know…"

"Mom, please," Arianna pleaded.

Gabby grabbed my hand. "Mommy, please. We never get to do anything cool like this. We'll be famous at school."

"I don't usually let my girls go off with—"

"A stranger?" Memphis laughed. "I get that. I sense you are a good mom. You should be, girl. You never know what's out there." She looked over her shoulder and waved one of her bodyguards over. "This is Marcus. He's one of my many bodyguards. He used to be a Navy SEAL."

"Hi, Marcus." I smiled at the large man. "Nice to meet you."

"Nice to meet you, miss." He nodded but didn't smile. He was broad and wore a black suit and dark sunglasses. His hair was cut short in a military style, and his demeanor matched his body language.

"Marcus would be able to transport the girls to my personal RV at the event. It's state-of-the-art. They could stay with me while I get ready. And I could show them around backstage."

"Oh, Mom, please." Arianna looked at me like I held the answers to the universe.

"Mommy! Please." Gabby joined in and clapped her hands together. "This is a once in a lifetime opportunity. Plus, it will make everyone at school so jealous!"

"I don't know." I shifted in my seat and set my teacup down. "I hate to accept because I know how busy you must be. There's all that getting ready and setting up on stage."

"It's no bother at all." She sighed and leaned back in her chair. "It would do me good to have some company while everything is being set up. I'll practice in the morning, so by the time they get there that afternoon, I can spend all my time with them. She cocked her head. "It's almost like you'll be doing me a favor." Her grin widened.

"Pleeeeaaasse," Arianna and Gabby said in unison with their hands pressed together under their chins.

It was a chance of a lifetime. And I wouldn't have to worry about Stephanie staying with the girls until I got my photos for the assignment that Uncle Stan had given me. Maybe all my reasons for not doing it were simply because I had trust issues. Besides, the girls would have security and safety while they were with Memphis. They would be as safe as the gold at Fort Knox.

"Well…" I looked at my girls, who were literally holding their breath.

"Are you sure it's no trouble?" I studied Memphis. Her face brightened with delight.

"Of course, not! And I will protect them as if they were my own." She nodded.

"Well, I suppose they can go."

The girls let out a squeal of laughter that drew several glances to our table.

"Perfect!" Memphis clasped perfectly manicured hands together. "If you will give me your cell phone number, I will send a text when Marcus is on his way over to pick them up."

I quickly told her my digits, which she promptly put into her phone. Then she stood.

"I can't wait for tomorrow. And I hope you enjoy the rest of your tea together." She waved and headed out the door with her security detail in tow.

CHAPTER 19

*T*hat night after the girls had gone to bed in our hotel room, I stepped out into the hallway to call Uncle Stan.

"Everything is still a go," Uncle Stan said. "You should be in the Peabody bar around six thirty tomorrow. Apparently, the husband likes to start drinking early. Don't get all dressed up. You don't want to outshine our bait girl."

"I'll be in jeans and a T-shirt." It was what I was going to wear to the concert. I had planned on getting my pictures and then heading over to the show afterwards.

"Perfect. And don't sit at the bar. You need to be seated in an area where you can take pictures of him and the woman without being noticed."

"But won't someone see that I have a camera?"

"Yes. But you'll have to blend in. Like you are getting ready to go sightseeing or something. I don't know. Make something up if someone asks why you have a camera. Although, I doubt anyone will. You need to be more concerned about getting that damn picture."

"I'll get it." I nodded.

"You better," he said gruffly. "I just had another call from someone who wants your job. Says he can get any picture, anywhere. He's new to Charming and is looking for work."

"Well, you don't need to hire anyone else. I have this job covered, as well as any other projects you need me to work on." I lifted my head with confidence.

"Even if I need you to work on a case for Nikki?"

A chill ran down my back. He didn't know I had followed her to his office.

"What kind of case would Nikki possibly need a private investigator for?" I snorted.

"She wants to find her husband."

"But didn't Brad leave a suicide note? I mean, it's more than likely he followed through on whatever he wrote in the letter." I tried to keep my voice calm and even, despite the fact that I didn't feel that way. Khalan had killed Brad when Brad shot me in the head for messing things up for him and Nikki. Lucky for me, a bullet to the brain couldn't kill a vampire. Khalan claimed to have gotten rid of the body and Brad's truck, all of which had my DNA on it.

But it still made me very uneasy that Nikki was now looking for proof.

"She needs a body for the life insurance."

"I'm sure she does," I gritted out between my clenched teeth.

"After you took your husband to the cleaners, I'm sure she figured she needed to start supporting herself."

"Until she finds another asshole to leach off of. Besides, are you sure that Miles and Nikki aren't still sleeping together?" I blurted it out. If anyone knew, Uncle Stan would. He was like Google.

"I'm sure. He's too damn busy working all the time for her now." He chortled. "I have to say, Rachel. I thought you wouldn't be wondering what your husband does and who he does it with by now."

"I am over it," I lied. I was mostly over it.

"Well, right now, I'm working on some leads concerning Brad. If something comes up where I need some pictures of something, I will let you know." He hung up.

I sat there looking at my cell phone for a few seconds. I hoped Uncle Stan could find enough evidence of Brad being dead without needing a body. That would be the best outcome for all of this. While I was sad that Brad had been killed, I was happier about being alive and Khalan taking care of Brad so I didn't have to look over my shoulder for the rest of my life.

Khalan.

I shook my head and headed back into my room. I had a job to do tomorrow, and I wasn't going to let Uncle Stan down.

CHAPTER 20

*T*he girls woke up ridiculously early. They were so excited to be spending the afternoon with Memphis that I barely got them to sit still long enough to eat breakfast. We still had hours until they were due to be picked up, and they had so much energy that I decided to do a quick walking tour of downtown Memphis.

"When are Mary Beth and her mom going to be here?" Arianna licked her ice cream cone. I had given in and let them eat ice cream for lunch. I figured since this was a special occasion, we should all celebrate.

I stifled a yawn behind my hand. The good thing about the girls being picked up at three was that I could catch a nap before I had to get ready for my job.

"I talked to them this morning. They are leaving later than planned and will meet us at the concert."

"Did you tell them about us meeting Memphis and how she invited us to visit with her this afternoon?" Arianna beamed.

"I did." I took a drink of the bitter coffee I had ordered. I really didn't want it. Since being turned into a vampire I wasn't that hungry for human food anymore. But I made an effort to eat in front of my girls.

"Were they so jealous?" Gabby laughed.

"Not exactly." I avoided their gazes.

"Why not?" Arianna snorted.

"Well, Stephanie thinks that I shouldn't have agreed to let you guys go since Memphis is technically a stranger." I had bristled during the conversation I had with Stephanie. She always made me feel like a failure as a mom. She seemed to have such high standards, ones that I could never reach. I was still surprised that she was even taking her daughter to the concert at all.

"She's so uncool," Arianna said.

"Arianna. That's not nice. Don't say things like that." I frowned at her.

"What? It's not like you weren't thinking it, too." She looked at me.

Maybe I was, but I wasn't going to say it.

I sighed. "Stephanie just has really high expectations, and sometimes people can't meet those expectations."

"I know. Mary Beth says all the time that her mom drives her crazy. She says she is indoctrinating her instead of letting her form her own opinions." Arianna took another lick of her cone.

"Well, let me tell you girls something. When you both become moms, you will see how hard a job it is."

"It won't be hard for me." Gabby licked her chocolate scoop. "I'm going to live in a castle and have twelve children."

"Twelve?" I stopped and stared at her.

"Yeah. That way, we can play all the time, and I will teach them cool things like sword fighting and how to ride a dragon and how to do Krav Maga."

"Krav Maga?" I stared at my daughter.

"Yeah. How else can you take down your enemies?" She blinked and took another lick.

I burst out laughing.

"I'm not having twelve children. I might not have any." Arianna shrugged.

"Neither of you should even be thinking about that right now. You have a lot of time before you make that decision. You need to graduate from school, settle on a career, go to college, get married…" It made me a little sad that my girls were growing up. I never thought about how quickly time passed, but here we were, talking about adult things and growing closer each second to the day when they wouldn't need me anymore.

"I wish the wizard was here with us. I bet he'd love to see Memphis. I bet he'd think Memphis was a beautiful princess," Gabby offered.

I cringed. "First of all, he's not a wizard. Secondly, I don't think he would like her music. I'm not so sure he'd like her."

"Oh, he'd like her, all right. All men like Memphis," Arianna said.

"Well, Khalan is not all men." I snorted.

"That's right." Gabby lifted her chin in the air. "He's different. He's a wizard. He has no time for romance."

Arianna rolled her eyes at her sister, but I didn't correct her. I was too busy thinking way too much about whether Khalan would find Memphis attractive. She seemed too bubbly and extroverted for him. But she was stunningly beautiful in a way that few women were.

"Now, I have another surprise for you girls. I booked us manicures back at the hotel."

"Really?" Ariana gave me a grateful look. "I didn't have time to paint my nails before we left." She held out her hand in front of her and examined her nails.

"Can I pick out what color I get to have?" Gabby looked at me under her lashes.

"As long as it's not something weird," Arianna said.

"What constitutes weird?" Gabby gave her an assessing look.

"Like Puke Green or Dragon Dung." Arianna shrugged.

"Arianna, those are not real names of nail polish."

"Well, they should be because she always picks out the ugliest colors," Arianna said.

"I'm just creative and don't live by other people's expectations. Besides, Dragon Dung is a cool name for a nail color. It would frighten off my sworn enemies of old." Gabby turned her attention back to her ice cream.

"See. You even talk weird. Enemies of old? Who says that?" Arianna wrinkled her nose in unveiled disgust.

"I bet Khalan does. 'Cause he's a wizard," Gabby answered without flinching.

I did a bad job of stifling my laugh.

"So, while we are on the subject of the Unabomber..." Arianna cut her eyes at me.

"Wizard," Gabby corrected.

"What exactly is going on between you two? Are you dating him?" Arianna continued, her hawk-like gaze trained on me as if I were a field mouse.

"No! Nothing is going on with us," I said quickly. "He's the gardener."

"Who just happened to defend you against Dad and carries you to the bedroom where he does God knows what," Arianna deadpanned.

"Arianna!" My mouth just about hit the sidewalk.

"What? Would you let the gardener carry *me* around?" She eyed me.

Gabby stopped eating her ice cream and waited for my answer.

I sighed. "Look. I'm going to be honest with you guys."

"You two are dating, aren't you?" Arianna looked horrified.

"No! Absolutely not." I glared.

"Darn. I wanted to have a wizard as a stepfather," Gabby pouted.

I shook my head. This conversation had taken a turn for the worse.

"Listen to me. Both of you. I am not dating Khalan or anyone else for that matter. When I get to that stage, I will let you know. As for what my relationship is with Khalan, he's just a friend."

Arianna rolled her eyes.

"He is, just a friend. I promise. He's been there for me in ways that others haven't."

"You mean like Daddy." Arianna cocked her head.

I shook my head and walked over to the bench and sat. I waved them over. They sat and stared at me.

"When I was going through the divorce, I didn't have much of a support system. Khalan showed up and, without me asking, helped in ways I didn't know I needed."

"Like replanting the penis flower garden?" Gabby said brightly. A woman passing by shot me a dirty look.

"Honey, let's stop referring to it like that." The night I had discovered Miles' affair, the flowerbed project which was supposed to look like the mascot for Ole Miss had ended up looking like a giant penis with blue balls. "But, yes. Khalan did replant the flowerbed. As well as checked on me from time to time to make sure I didn't need anything."

"In exchange for what?" Arianna narrowed her eyes.

"For nothing." I blinked. "Well, except to help him with some coyote pups whose mom had been shot."

"Who would shoot a mama coyote?" Gabby's lips quivered.

"Some hunters who were doing it for sport."

"Did the babies live?" Arianna asked quietly.

"They did. And they are going to be fine now."

"But who's taking care of them? Why didn't you bring them home?" Gabby asked.

"Another pack took them in." I didn't dare say it was a werewolf Pack. "And I couldn't bring them home because they are wild. They need to be with their own kind."

"That's all he's ever asked you to do?" Arianna raised a brow.

"Yes. So, you see, there's nothing going on between us. Besides, I don't think he dates."

"No, I don't imagine he would," Gabby said thoughtfully.

"What do you mean?" I settled my gaze on my youngest.

"I mean, he's clearly the kind of guy who only loves one person. He's faithful and honorable. And a whole lot scary. That's a good thing." Gabby nodded. "Plus, he's a wizard."

"Gabby…" I wanted to say that none of those things were true. Most of all that he wasn't a wizard. But I was tired and just wanted to get back to the hotel where it was dark, and we could get manicures.

I glanced at the time on my watch.

"Let's head back so we can get our nails done."

CHAPTER 21

"*Y*ou girls mind your manners. And call me if you need me." I hugged Arianna tightly and then Gabby. I looked up at Marcus, who stood holding the car door open with a stern expression that never changed.

"Mommy, we won't call you. We'll be having too much fun." Gabby's eyes sparkled.

"Here, take a picture of me getting picked up." Arianna handed me her phone. She struck a pose beside Marcus, who didn't flinch.

I snapped the picture and handed the phone back to her. I looked at Gabby. "Do you want me to take a picture of you with Marcus."

"Nah. I'll wait until we get on Memphis's tour bus." She waggled her eyebrows.

I shook my head. I hoped I was doing the right thing by letting my girls go. Stephanie's words kept coming to mind. She'd said that Memphis was a stranger and had warned against letting Gabby and Arianna go.

"Stop worrying, Mom." Arianna gave me a look. "We'll see

you in a few hours. Besides, like you said, we will call if we need you to come sooner."

"I know. I know. I can't help but worry. You are my life." I brushed my hand across their dark hair.

"Ma'am, we need to get going before the traffic gets bad," Marcus said in his monotone voice.

"Okay." I gave them each one last hug and kiss then watched from the sidewalk as they climbed into the back seat of the blacked-out Suburban. "Put your seat belts on," I reminded.

Marcus shut the door behind them. He gave me a nod.

I watched as the black SUV pulled onto Memphis street and drove out of sight. I couldn't help the lump that built in my throat. I tried to swallow, but my throat was tight and dry. I walked back inside the Peabody and out of the bright sun.

I started to go upstairs because I was tired and needed a nap before I started to work, but I knew if I were alone upstairs, I wouldn't be able to sleep, wondering if the girls were okay. I stopped in front of the standing display of the Peabody's spa services. My gaze stopped at the description of the full body massage.

I decided to walk over to the spa and see if they had an opening.

It was dark and calming and instantly made me feel at ease.

"May I help you?" The receptionist was an older woman with kind eyes.

"Yes. I don't have an appointment, but I was hoping to get a full body massage."

"What room are you in?" She looked at her computer screen.

"The Presidential Suite."

"Ah. That's one of our nicer rooms. Although, I have to

say, all the rooms at the Peabody are nice." She smiled and began clicking some keys on the keyboard.

"I'm sorry about the short notice."

"Not at all. In fact, we have an opening right now with Zena." She looked up from the screen.

"Perfect. I'll take it."

The receptionist stood from behind the desk and walked me over to the changing room. "Here's a locker for you to put all your items in, and here are the robes and slippers." She pointed to a basket of slippers and the shelf of neatly rolled-up robes. "After you've changed into the robe, someone will come and get you for your appointment. And, remember, when you're done, be sure to drink lots of water to get all those toxins out of your system."

"Thank you." I watched her exit the room. I picked up a pair of slippers and a robe then snagged the key off the locker and headed into the bathroom to change.

When I came out, I locked my belongings in the storage unit and wrapped the bungie keychain around my wrist.

I sat down in one of the oversized chairs and looked around. Soft music played, and the lights were dim. A carafe of ice water and glasses sat on a long table, along with a lit candle.

A soft water feature rested against one wall, and it would have put me to sleep if I weren't so anxious about my children.

The door opened, and a young woman in her twenties stepped inside. She was tall and blond with perfect skin.

"You must be Mrs. Jones. I'm Zena. I'll be doing your massage today," she said with a smile and gestured. "Right this way."

I followed her down the dark hallway into one of the small rooms. "I'll leave you to disrobe and climb under the sheets. I'll start with the front side, so lay on your back, please. You can hang your robe on the hook." She shut the door behind her as she left.

I shoved the key to the locker into my pocket and disrobed. I was naked except for my panties. Even when I was human, I'd always kept my underwear on whenever I got a massage.

I climbed under the warm blankets and lay down on my back. The room was warm, and the darkness made my body relax.

The door opened with a soft knock, and Zena stepped inside. "Do you have any areas that you want me to focus on?"

"Not really. Just all over, I suppose. And you can do deep tissue. I'm hard to hurt." I closed my eyes.

I heard her pumping oil into her hand, followed by the unmistakable sound of her rubbing her palms together. She stood at my head and placed her hands on either side of my neck and began to rub.

My mind drifted as she worked her magic on my body. It had been too long since I'd had human touch other than a hug from my daughters. Maybe that's why I had started getting turned on by Khalan. Perhaps I needed to go on a date.

I could not believe my girls thought that Khalan and I were a thing. They didn't know him like I did. Khalan would never be with anyone, let alone me. It seemed like too much effort on his part. He'd rather be living in the wild with animals than anywhere with humans.

I sighed as Zena made her way down my body to my legs. After a while, she softly whispered for me to turn over onto my stomach. I placed my face in the soft donut and relaxed as she started working on my neck. Between the massage and the dark room, I felt myself relax deeper until I fell asleep.

I dreamed that I was in a bedroom with Khalan. He was

shirtless and standing in the middle of the room, staring at me. His midsection was ripped with muscles like a warrior, and his hair hung around his face. His dark eyes focused on me and made my belly warm.

"Come here." He crooked his finger at me.

Desire rushed through me like a river, and I couldn't stop. I took one step and then another until I was standing inches away from his large body.

"Khalan." I whispered his name.

He reached out his hand and cupped my cheek. Such a small gesture, but it sent my libido into overdrive. My heart thumped loudly in my chest, and my body ached.

He leaned in, and I held my breath. He was going to kiss me. I knew it.

My lips parted, and I closed my eyes.

"Rachel," he said my name.

"Yes." I begged him without words to press his lips to mine, to ease the ache that had built between my legs.

"Wake the fuck up."

I bolted upright. I blinked and looked around the dark space.

I was in the massage room. I glanced at my reflection in the mirror. My face had crease marks where I had been face-down in the donut, and my hair was sticking up in all directions. I looked like I had escaped the nut house.

I scooted off the table and took the sheet with me. I quickly put the robe on and peeked out into the hallway. It was empty, so I made my way back to the room where I had undressed.

I stuck the key in my locker and grabbed my clothes then looked at my watch. My heart almost stopped.

It was almost six o'clock. I was supposed to be in the bar and set up by six thirty.

I hurried and dressed. I glanced at the mirror and patted

down my hair. I raced out of the room and headed to the front desk.

"How was your massage?" The receptionist smiled at me.

"It was great. Is there any way I can put this on my room?" I glanced at my watch again.

"Of course." She typed something into the computer. "Do you want a receipt?"

"No. That's okay." I smiled and hurried out of the spa. I found the nearest elevator and pressed the button. I made a mental note to pay this before checking out so Uncle Sam wouldn't know.

I tapped my foot impatiently as I waited for the doors to open. To my relief, they finally peeled apart, and my stomach dropped. It was full. I had to wait until everyone got off before I stepped inside.

I pressed the button, and the doors finally slid together.

"Hold the elevator," a woman's voice called out. She stuck her hand in between the doors before it had a chance to shut.

I reluctantly pressed the open button and stifled a growl.

"Thanks." She stepped inside and rolled her luggage behind her.

"What floor?" I asked.

"Fourth," she said.

I rolled my eyes. That was two floors below mine, which meant it was going to take longer to get to my room and grab my camera.

"Don't you just love the Peabody?" The woman dressed in a pink suit smiled. Her Southern drawl was evident, and it made me think of Charleston.

"I do." I smiled and glanced at my watch again. The elevator seemed to be moving at a turtle's pace.

"Do you stay here often?" she asked as she patted the string of pearls around her neck.

"Whenever I get the chance. I'm here with my daughters

for the Memphis in Memphis concert." I smiled politely and looked at the floor number we were at.

"Oh, yes. I hear that it's such a big turnout. I'm not one for her music, but it seems like she has quite the following." She smiled again.

"Yes. So it would seem." I breathed out a sigh of relief when the doors to the fourth floor opened.

"Have a nice evening." She waved and stepped off.

As soon as she was clear of the doors, I pressed the close button and hit my floor number again.

When it appeared up top, and the elevator opened, I sprinted down the hall to my room.

CHAPTER 22

I managed to grab my camera and change into a pink T-shirt with the words *Soccer Mom* scripted across the front in black letters. I kept my jeans and sneakers on because I didn't want to waste time changing them when those minutes could be used to put on makeup.

I didn't even have time for that. I ended up putting on some mascara and pink lip gloss and running out the door.

By the time I made it downstairs, the lobby bar was getting crowded. I flirted shameless with the bartender and told him I was desperate for a table in the corner. He grinned and escorted me to the exact one I wanted. Before he left, his hand lingered on my lower back.

Instinct wanted me to slap his face, but I didn't need to cause a scene. I needed to blend in.

I smiled seductively and took the napkin with his number scribbled across and promised to call.

I watched him retreat back behind the bar and shoved the napkin into a nearby garbage can.

I sat in the chair and looked around the room. I set my

oversized Louis Vuitton bag on the table and pulled out my camera, placing it on the table beside my purse.

I scanned the room and the bar area. Right now, there were a bunch of businessmen in suits sitting at the bar drinking beer and talking animatedly.

I pulled out Jonathan Lender's photo and looked at it. After studying his picture, I slipped it back into my purse. I looked around the room again, searching for my mark.

I sipped on my glass of white wine that the bartender had poured for me and studied the room.

My breath nearly slipped out of my lungs when I spotted him.

He strutted into the room and headed straight for the bar. He wasn't attractive, and his beer belly made him even less so.

I didn't like the looks of him.

I sipped my glass of wine and waited for him to sit. He eased onto one of the barstools at the bar and waved the bartender over. The guy put some ice in a tumbler and poured what appeared to be Scotch over the cubes.

Jonathan didn't waste time, he immediately drained his glass then patted the bar, indicating for the bartender to give him another.

I could tell that the bartender was trying to be pleasant. But the tense lines around his eyes and mouth suggested that he knew Jonathan's type and was mentally preparing himself for the drunken antics of an entitled asshole.

Jonathan turned on the barstool and looked around the room, sizing up the women. I ducked my head and suddenly became interested in texting on my phone. I knew he didn't know who I was, but I didn't need him coming over to me to try and hit on me. I needed to stay invisible and get the picture.

The buzz of voices seemed to vibrate around me like anxious bees. I took another big sip of my wine and glanced up. Jonathan had turned his attention back to a blonde who had slipped into the seat next to him. I couldn't see the woman's face to recognize if this was the bait woman or not. She was blond, but her figure seemed larger. And she didn't have on anything sexy. Just a pair of tan slacks and a flowered top.

Something about the woman was familiar, but I couldn't put my finger on what.

Jonathan moved in closer to the blonde, and whatever she said had him laughing. He moved his seat closer and slid his arm around the back of her barstool.

The bartender delivered a glass of red wine to the woman, and she began leaning into Jonathan.

I moved the camera on the table and leaned down to see if I had it positioned correctly, and the image was clear and not fuzzy. Pleased, I sat up and pressed the button. I clicked a few more pictures. I needed to get a shot of him kissing this woman, not just flirting. I glanced over at the bar and waited. Whatever the woman had said to Jonathan had him waving the bartender over so he could pay the bill. He scribbled on the receipt and slid off the barstool. He looked around and then helped the woman gather her purse. She looked at the floor and smiled before her hair curtained her face.

Something about her looked so very familiar.

I stood up and gathered my purse and camera. I laid a twenty on the table for my wine, and discretely followed them out.

The woman dropped her room key and bent to pick it up. When she stood, Jonathan pressed her into a dark corner and kissed her.

My heart raced in my chest. Here was my chance. I picked up the camera and aimed it at them. I snapped a picture. The man stiffened and broke the kiss. He looked directly at me. I continued snapping shots. Not only did I have a picture of him kissing another woman that wasn't his wife, but I also had a clear shot of his face.

"Rachel?" The woman stepped out of the corner.

I blinked.

Shit. It was Carla. My neighbor.

"Wait, you know her?" Jonathan shoved his thumb in my direction.

"Rachel, what are you doing here?" Carla ran her hand down her short, blond hair and looked at the floor. "You're not going to tell Cal I was kissing another man, are you?"

"Cal? Who the fuck is Cal?" Jonathan thundered.

"I'm here for the concert." I shoved my camera into my purse and slung it over my shoulder. "I'm taking the girls to see Memphis in Memphis." My voice trembled a little.

"What are you doing with that camera?" Carla's eyes darted to my purse.

"It's for the concert," I lied.

"Who the hell are you?" Jonathan took a step in my direction. His face had shifted into something mean, almost evil. It made the hair on my neck stand up.

"She's Rachel Jones. My neighbor," Carla blurted out. Her eyes were wide and afraid.

"Why were you taking my picture?" Jonathan narrowed his eyes on me.

"I wasn't taking a picture. I was just making sure it was set up and ready for the concert tonight." I glanced at my watch. "I need to be going, or I'll be late." I turned to leave.

Jonathan grabbed my arm. "You're not going anywhere, bitch."

I spun around and snatched my arm out of his grasp. "Don't put your hands on me."

"I can do whatever I want." His lips curled into an evil grin. "If you are Carla's neighbor, are you into hooking up

with strangers in a bar, too? I'd be more than happy to entertain both of you ladies tonight."

"I'm not interested." I curled my fingers into fists. I
wanted to plow one of them into the guy's ugly, smug face.

"Rachel, you're not going to tell Cal, are you?" Carla
stepped between Jonathan and me.

"Tell Cal? How the hell am I going to tell Cal? He's in
prison." I took a step back. I had felt so bad for Carla after
Cal's arrest. I'd thought she was just an innocent housewife
who had fallen on hard times due to her shitty husband. But
here she was, hooking up with some random man.

"Whoa." Jonathan took a step back. "You didn't say you
were married to a jailbird."

"Technically, he's not had his trial yet. So, I'm not sure the
term *jailbird* fits." Carla blinked.

"I have to be going. You two have a good night." I turned
and headed toward the valet. I could have gone back to my
room for a while, but I didn't want to be in the same building
with Carla right now.

I'd felt sorry for her when Cal had been arrested for
murder. But not now. She had no qualms about sleeping with
a married man while she was still legally married herself.
Even if she was hitched to a murderer.

"Rachel, wait," Carla called after me.

I walked out the door. The valet smiled at me.

"I need my car, please. I'm in the Presidential Suite."

"Right away." He grabbed my key and jogged off in the
direction of the parking garage.

"Rachel, please." Carla caught up to me and touched my
shoulder.

"What?" I turned around and glared.

"It's not what it seems," she said quietly.

"Really? 'Cause it looked like you had your tongue down

that douchebag's throat and were about to go back to his room for sex."

"I had to." She looked over her shoulder to see if Jonathan was following her. "He promised me money." She looked at my purse.

"You mean, you set up to meet him?"

"Yeah. It was arranged by this guy in Memphis. Sex for money."

I stared at her unblinking." You mean men pay for you to...."

"Have sex? Yes." She lifted her chin. "Just because I don't look like you doesn't mean men won't pay for it. Besides, some men like a woman with some meat on her bones and some experience." She ran her hand down her rounded stomach.

I was so shocked, I couldn't speak.

"Don't judge me, Rachel." Carla cocked her head. "What are you doing here? You really taking your girls to the Memphis concert?" She cocked her head more like she didn't believe me.

"Yes. I am." I crossed my arms over my chest.

"Then where are the girls?" She shot me a look that said she didn't believe me.

"They're already at the venue. We met Memphis here when we were having tea. She came over and started chatting. She offered to pick the girls up early so they could get a tour of behind the scenes and check out her tour bus."

Carla's eyes grew wide. "You let your underage children go on a tour bus?"

"It's not like she's a rock star. She's a country singer." I straightened my shoulders. I didn't need condemnation from someone like Carla.

"You have heard the rumors, right?" Her expression grew serious.

"What rumors?" My mouth dried up. Unease sauntered through my gut.

"There's a website that keeps up with Memphis. They say that at least one person always disappears at her concerts." She leaned in closer. "They say that she may be into human trafficking."

"What?" I shook my head. "Why the hell would she do that? She's a multimillionaire. She has properties all over the world. That doesn't make sense for her to do that."

"That's what she said too when asked about the disappearances in an interview." Carla shrugged. "I'm just telling you what I've heard."

"And is this the same website that said Hollywood is run by aliens from the planet Saturn?" I arched my brow.

"It's Uranus. Not Saturn. And no, that's a different site." She shook her head. "Look, I have to get back and see if he's still interested. Do me a favor and don't tell anyone you saw me here."

"Carla," I called after her, but she had already walked back inside.

"Perfect," I groused. I had to make a choice. Give the picture to Uncle Stan and keep my job. Or tell him I couldn't get the shot and have him replace me.

The valet drove up with my Volvo. "Here you go, ma'am." He held the driver's door open for me.

"Thank you." I dug around in my purse and pulled out a five-dollar bill. He thanked me and shut the door.

I pulled out onto the street with my anxiety at an all-time high.

CHAPTER 23

$\mathcal{B}$y the time I pulled into the parking area for the concert, it was dark. I tried telling the attendant at the gate that Memphis had my name written down for a special parking spot. He checked his list and, apparently, she had forgotten to add me.

So I ended up parking at the very end of the lot. I grabbed my purse and got out of the car. I opened the back of the Volvo and pulled out five travel chairs. I quickly changed out my purse for a much smaller one. Memphis had promised that we were in the area up front by the stage. I was going to go in and set up the chairs and then find my girls.

By the time I made it to the entrance, I had broken out in a thin sheen of sweat. I handed the guy my ticket, and he waved me in.

I looked around the crowd of young people and suddenly felt very old. A few moms milled about taking selfies with their daughters in shirts they had decorated themselves with Memphis splashed across the front. I glanced down at my appearance and felt very shabby compared to everyone else.

I cringed at the drone of voices that seemed to carry on in

the dark. I squinted at the stage and wanted to let out a string of curses. I hiked up my purse on one shoulder and the travel chairs in their respective bags on the other.

"Hey, baby." A guy that appeared to be in his twenties stumbled into me, reeking of beer.

"Excuse me," I groused.

"Where ya going? You can come sit by me," he called. He drug his gaze up from my breasts to my face. "Hey Mrs. Jones. Looking hot."

"Ricky Spencer." I fisted my hands at my side. He was my neighbor's kid with a sportscar and an overinflated ego.

"The offer still stands. You can come sit by me and I can show you what a real man is like." He grinned.

"Not a chance in hell." I muttered. I continued my trek, picking through the crowd of people.

Two large screens were situated on either side of the stage with giant videos of Memphis in different poses. Each one flashed a different sexy picture of Memphis in different sequined outfits.

My gut twisted. This was not at all what I had pictured for a concert for the girls. It was way more sexy than I'd anticipated. I had listened to Memphis's songs on the radio. I figured since all the teenagers liked her, she would present herself to that demographic. But the pictures on the big screens told me a different story. I picked up the pace and hurried to the front of the stage. When I got there, I spotted a section roped off with guards standing on either side.

"Hi. I have a reserved spot from Memphis. My name is Rachel Jones. There should be five spots." I looked at the man wearing all black.

He pulled out his cell phone and made a call. After a few short words, he held up the rope and motioned me through.

I ducked and caught the end of my chair on the rope. I struggled for a few seconds before getting untangled.

"Over there." He motioned with his hand toward the middle of the stage.

"Thanks." I narrowed my eyes on him. I was not impressed with the hospitality of Memphis's team.

I set about the task of setting up the chairs. When I was done, I stood up straight and whipped my sweaty hair out of my face. I propped my hands on my hips and looked around.

I pulled my cell phone out of my purse and dialed Arianna. When she didn't answer, I called Gabby's phone.

"Rachel!"

I turned around at the sound of my name. It was Stephanie.

I hung up the phone when Gabby didn't answer.

"Hey, come on over." I nodded to the security guard that it was okay to let her in.

She eyed him warily and lifted the rope. She and Mary Beth had to duck low to get under.

"I figured you'd be here already," I said, looking around the crowd. "I brought extra chairs for you guys."

"Oh. Thanks. I completely forgot about that." She smiled and looked down at Mary Beth, who was taking in the whole scene. I was sure she'd never been to anything like this before. "Where are Arianna and Gabby."

My gut twisted. I hated to tell her that I had no idea. So, I lied. "They are on the tour bus with Memphis. I'm going to go get them. Do you mind staying with the chairs?"

"Not at all." She smiled.

"Can I go? I want to meet Memphis," Mary Beth pleaded.

"Sur…"

"Absolutely not," Stephanie snapped. My friend looked at me and gave me a sheepish grin. "Sorry. I'm just really protective of who Mary Beth is around."

Mary Beth's face fell. She looked like someone had stolen her puppy.

"I see." I hiked my purse up high on my shoulder and ducked under the rope.

Irritation that Stephanie thought I was a bad mother coupled with the fact that Arianna and Gabby were both ignoring my phone calls had me on edge.

I scanned the crowd to see if I could see the tour bus.

I couldn't.

I debated going back to the security guard and asking where it was, but then I spotted Marcus in the crowd.

I ran in his direction, holding tight to my purse.

"Marcus!" I screamed.

Either he didn't hear me, or he was ignoring me.

I clutched my purse like a shield across my chest and sprinted toward him. If I lost him now in the crowd, I knew I would never find him again.

I bumped into numerous people, but I didn't care. I needed to find my girls.

The bodyguard walked behind the stage. I tried to follow, but two security guards blocked me.

"You can't go back there." One of the men dressed in black held up his hand.

"You don't understand. My daughters are with Memphis. I need to get to them." I stretched and looked around the massive man. Marcus had stepped into one of the mega-tour buses.

"What's your name?" He cocked his head.

"Rachel. Rachel Jones."

He pulled out his phone and sent a quick text. Within seconds, it dinged with a reply. "Sorry, ma'am. No one has heard of you. You need to leave."

My face heated, and my stomach churned.

"No. I will not. I want my children, or I am going to call the police." Panic welled inside of me. I felt like I was alone and helpless. I pulled out my phone.

"Wait." Marcus stepped out from behind the security guard. "Mrs. Jones. If you will just come with me."

The first step I took, I nearly stumbled with relief.

"Thank you, Marcus." I followed at his side. "I was beginning to get worried."

"Sorry about that, Mrs. Jones. Those guys are not privy to what Memphis has going on. They are local security mainly hired to keep people away from backstage and the tour bus."

I pressed my hand over my heart and slowed my breathing. We walked over to the large maroon and black tour bus parked several yards from the backstage area. Two men stood on either side of the door. They opened it when Marcus approached.

"Go on in. I believe your girls are inside." He waved me inside.

"Thank you, Marcus." I hurried up the steps and inside the massive RV.

I was immediately hit with a rush of cool air. I sighed, relieved that the air conditioning was on and running cold. I got to the top of the stairs and looked around the large living room and kitchen—at least big for something on wheels. The floors and countertops were white and gray marble. High-end stainless-steel appliances were in the kitchen. And the couches were soft, white leather.

A massive TV, currently on, hung above the electric fireplace.

"Hello?" I walked into the kitchen. Soft music came from the back of the bus. I made my way past the bathroom and bunk beds. The door was closed to the main bedroom.

I knocked. "Hello? Arianna? Gabby? Are you guys in there?"

The door swung open, and Memphis stood there with a surprised look on her face.

"Rachel. I wasn't expecting you so soon."

I glanced at my watch and frowned. "Actually, I'm late. I said I would be here earlier, but the traffic was horrendous, and so was trying to find a parking spot."

I looked over her shoulder. "Where are Arianna and Gabby?"

"They're taking a nap. They had such a long day, they are exhausted." She gave me a saccharine smile.

The hair on the back of my neck stood at attention. "Well, if it's all the same to you, I'll just check on them." I shoved past her when she tried to block me. She was stronger than she looked for a young woman. But I was older, a vampire, and a mother. It wasn't a fair fight.

My breath caught in my throat. I smelled the coppery scent of blood in the air before I saw the tiny drop on the white bedding. My girls were lying on the bed, a small pool of blood under their cheeks.

"Oh my God. What happened?" I rushed to their sides and knelt. I could hear their heartbeats. They were slow but strong.

"Arianna?" I cradled her face in my hands.

"Mom?" she mumbled but kept her eyes closed.

I ran my hands over her face to determine where the blood was coming from. My fingertips found the sticky patch of blood on her neck.

"What have you done? What have you done?" I screamed at Memphis.

I went to Gabby and brushed the hair out of her face. She blinked and tried to speak, but nothing came out.

They were both dazed and groggy.

"What did you do to them?" I glared at Memphis.

"I glamoured them so I could taste their blood." Her full lips curled into a perfect, evil smile.

Holy fuck.

"You're a vampire." The words dropped from my mouth like an atomic bomb.

"And I know who you are." Her eyes tightened and flared. "You see, you have something I've been missing."

"What is that?" I stood and placed myself between Memphis and my children. No way in hell was this bitch going to hurt my kids again.

She went to the wall and pressed a button. A door slid back and revealed a secret room. My breath caught in my throat. "Khalan."

He was spread crucifix-like with his arms nailed to either side of the wall. He was bare-chested, and blood seeped from his mouth onto his muscular pecs. His long, black hair was matted to his head.

"What did you do to him?"

"You should be asking what he did to *me*." She crossed her arms over her chest and glared at me.

"How do you know Khalan?" My throat began to tighten.

"I'm his Maker." She sneered.

"Maker? But you look way younger than he does."

"So? I've been around a lot longer than Khalan. In fact, I was one of the first vampires in Europe."

"What?" I felt the blood drain from my face.

"No. You Americans are so stupid. You will believe anything posted on social media." She shook her head and walked over to the small refrigerator on the other side of the room. She pulled out a chilled red wine glass and poured a dark liquid into it. The smell of cold blood filled the room. She took a sip and delicately wiped the corners of her mouth with her fingertips.

"What do you want with my children?" I tracked her as she walked back over to Khalan.

"I needed them to get to my progeny." You see, when I saw

you at the Peabody, I could smell Khalan's blood on you. As his Maker, I have that connection. I knew the only way I could get Khalan to come back to me was to get you or someone close to you." She glanced at the girls then smiled. "And I was right. The second I glamoured the girls, I could hear Khalan trying to get to them." She frowned and looked at me. "They are not vampires. Yet Khalan has exchanged blood with them."

"He what?" I looked at him.

"Oh, did he not tell you?" She laughed. "How positively amusing. I wonder what else he hasn't told you." She walked over and traced a nail down his chest. Blood pooled and dripped from the cut.

"I was born in France and lived in different countries. My father was a wealthy aristocrat, and we traveled all the time. When I was twenty-one, I wanted to be a singer. I was bored with all the parties we went to all the time, and I had a wonderful voice. But my father wouldn't allow it. One night, as we traveled by coach, someone pulled us over and robbed us. The highwayman killed both of my parents by ripping out their throats, but he spared my life. He then told me he would give me anything I could ever want. In exchange, I would be his bride."

I watched as Memphis told the story. It gave me chills, but her expression never changed.

"I'm sorry he killed your parents." I put myself between the vampire and my children.

Her eyes sparkled with excitement. "I wasn't." She turned her dead eyes on me. "They never let me do anything fun. They were always trying to ruin my life."

"I'm sure they were protecting you. Like all good parents do," I added.

"No, they weren't. They were horrible parents." Her eyes went dark. "They wanted to control me. To tell me how to live my life." She curled her fingers around the wine glass.

"That night on the highway, a stranger set me free. A stranger named Adelmo."

"A vampire." I swallowed.

"More than a vampire. He was my savior." Her eyes glazed over as she remembered the past. "He gave me the life I was always destined to have." She lifted the glass to her lips and took a sip.

"He took away your life," I said softly.

She trained her eyes on me. "He gave me wealth, fame, and immortality. Who could ask for anything more?"

CHAPTER 24

a chill ran down my spine. "So, when did you turn Khalan?" I hoped to keep her talking to buy some time for me to figure out a way to get the hell out of this tour bus with my children.

"Khalan." She looked back at my Maker strung up on the wall. "Well, that's quite an interesting story."

"I'm sure."

Memphis walked toward Khalan. "You can't imagine what he looks like without this scruffy beard and long hair." She sighed. "When I met him, that's how he looked, clean-shaven and well respected. But I suppose most holy men are."

That knocked the breath out of me. "Are you trying to tell me that Khalan was a priest?"

"No, a country preacher in one of the New England states." She waved her hand dismissively in the air. "Massachusetts or Maine or one of those other tiny ones."

I looked at Khalan. No way could I imagine someone who hated humanity so much being a preacher in his former life as a human.

"I had gotten bored with Adelmo, so I got on a boat and

traveled to the United States. It was a new country, fresh with possibilities and new blood." She smirked.

"Wasn't Adelmo upset that you left? Didn't he try to follow you?"

"He couldn't very well do that with him being beheaded and all." She deadpanned.

My eyes widened. "You killed your Maker? I thought that was against the rules."

"Let me guess. You've been watching those vampire movies on TV." She barked out a laugh. "Apparently, Khalan hasn't been a very good Maker if he didn't explain the rules." She arched an eyebrow.

"Let's just say I'm a very reluctant student." I looked over my shoulder to check on my girls. They were both still out of it but breathing regularly.

"So, how did you meet Khalan?" I turned the conversation back to Memphis, a subject I knew she liked talking about.

I was traveling through a village when I spotted him coming out of a small country church. He was greeting his congregation as they left, and I couldn't stop staring at him. I had never seen a more handsome man in my life." She took another drink and twirled a blond curl around her claw-like fingernail. "I hadn't planned to stay, but I found myself renting out a room in some old lady's house in town. I started going to church and watching him every time he stepped behind that pulpit. I didn't approach him. I knew he saw me, so I waited for him to come to me. Like all men do."

"What happened?"

Her lips flattened into an angry line. "I grew impatient, so I went to his house one night. It was a small dwelling, way in the country. Imagine my surprise when I knocked on the door, and someone else opened it."

"Who was it?" This was the most I had ever heard about

Khalan. He never told me anything about his life, and I couldn't help but be fascinated despite my fear.

"His pregnant wife."

"Wife? I never knew he was married." I looked over at Khalan. He'd raised his head a little, met my gaze, and then let it drop.

"Apparently, she had been on bed rest for the pregnancy. She asked me to come in when I said I was there to see Khalan. She thought I was looking for spiritual guidance. I was looking to satisfy another need instead."

"But he was married." I narrowed my eyes. With a family.

"So?" She shrugged. "I managed to get Khalan outside so we could talk. When we were alone, I confessed my feelings for him and told him that I wanted to be with him. He issued an argument, but once I kissed him, I could feel his resolve crumbling."

Nausea rose in my throat.

"I told him that we could leave and start a life together. I told him I was wealthy and said he could have anything he wanted. Even eternal life." Her expression shifted into something dark. "He said kissing me was a mistake, and that he loved his wife and he'd never leave her." She tightened her grip on the wine goblet. The glass shattered, spilling splinters and red wine over the floor of the tour bus. "Can you imagine? He said no to me."

"I guess you don't get turned down very much."

Her gaze snapped to me, and she glared. "I never get turned down. I always get everything I want. And I got what I wanted that night."

I didn't want to hear the rest of the story. I really didn't. All I wanted was to grab my children and run.

"I turned Khalan that night. And after he was turned, I glamoured him into draining his wife of blood. Once he realized what he had done, he became inconsolable. He refused to eat for weeks until I finally tied him down and forced blood down his throat. Once he was strong enough, he tried to kill me, but it was impossible. As his Maker, I could hear his thoughts, and I knew what he was going to do before he actually did it."

"A Maker can hear thoughts." I blinked. Holy shit.

"Of course. But only those of the vampires they create. And only when they are really weak from lack of blood."

"So, how did you and him part ways?"

"We parted ways when he stabbed me in the heart with a silver knife and trapped me in a silver-lined coffin. He buried me six feet under in a cemetery in Salem, Massachusetts. He figured the lack of blood and inability to get out of the coffin would kill me. He didn't plan on me being able to survive all those years until some funeral home worker dug me up. There was no marker for my grave, so while he was digging a new one, he found my coffin and opened it." She laughed. "I wish you could have seen his face when he saw me all shriveled up and impaled through the chest. The last thing he saw was me feasting on his body until nothing was left."

I shivered. "So, how did you find Khalan?"

A sinister smile grew on her lips. "Once I got out of Salem, I traveled all over the United States trying to find him. I had almost given up until one night, I felt him." She glared at me. "I felt him when he turned you into a vampire."

My mouth dropped open.

"It's a bond that Makers have with any vampire they turn. Once their progeny turns another, there's almost an echo that we can feel in our blood. I felt it on a night when it snowed in the South."

My knees buckled. I grabbed the wall to regain my balance.

She cocked her head. "After all those years of being alone, Khalan never turned another vampire. He survived on his own all that time...until you came along. Which made me realize that even though you are how I found him, you are now my biggest threat. And I don't like competition. Especially when it comes to my true love's heart." Her gaze narrowed like a snake's eyes.

"Wait. I think you've totally gotten the wrong idea about me and Khalan." I held out my hand. "Have I now? Why would he risk everything to turn you? And why would he give his blood to your children so he would always know where they are? It looks like a cozy family situation to me." She gritted her teeth.

"I assure you, it's not. Khalan can't stand me. He is constantly bitching about how much of a disappointment I am as a vampire." I slammed my mouth shut and looked over my shoulder at my children. They were both still sleeping, and I hoped they wouldn't remember any of this tomorrow.

"Besides, why would you even want to be with someone who staked you through the heart?"

"Khalan loves me. He does. He just doesn't realize it yet. He was mad when I made him kill his wife, but he's had time to get over that. And now that I've found him, we can be together. Like I always hoped." She hummed the tune to her song and ran a fingernail down Khalan's bare chest.

For the first time, I really listened to the words of the hit.

From the moment we met, you were my only desire.
I wished for love, and your eyes inspired.
It was to last forever until you broke my heart.
Now my view of the world has come up short.

I'm the Temptress from Memphis.
No one compares to me.
I'm your true love and soul mate,
The one you'll love in eternally.

Now I'm back, and I'm bitter,
   And you will worship at my feet.
   You'll beg me not to leave you.
   You will see your punishment is overdue.
   I'm the Temptress from Memphis.
   No one compares to me.
   I'm your true love and soul mate,
   The one you'll love in eternally.

There's no escape from my wrath,
   From my generous heart you threw away.
   It's my turn to show you what Hell looks like,
   When I turn my love away.

I looked at Memphis. "*Temptress from Memphis.* You wrote that about Khalan."

"Ding, ding, ding. You are smarter than you look." She took a step toward me.

I held up my hands. "So, all the stories about you are true? You kidnapping people from your concerts. You are killing them for their blood."

"Duh." She rolled her eyes. "Do you know how many young kids come to my show. I'd rather have young, vibrant blood instead of old, dried-up bitches like you."

I narrowed my eyes. "Khalan didn't think I was dried up."

Her eyes widened in anger. I had hit her where it hurt.

She lunged toward me and knocked us to the floor. She scrambled on top of me and bared her teeth then tightened her hands around my neck, squeezing off my air.

But I had another power that she didn't. I was a mother.

And I was a fighter. And it would be a cold day in Hell before I let another woman hurt my family.

I bucked Memphis off and got on top of her. She screamed.

I grabbed a handful of her blond hair and slammed her head into the floor. She grinned up at me evilly. "You stupid bitch. You can't kill me. I'm undead."

"But I can, you evil Whore of Babylon!" Stephanie came running toward us with a crucifix and what appeared to be a bottle of holy water.

I looked up, shocked to see her. It was my mistake. Memphis punched me hard in the mouth and knocked me off her.

"In the name of…" Stephanie didn't get to finish her battle cry before Memphis jumped to her feet.

"Are you fucking kidding me? You think you can take me?" Memphis snarled.

"I can in the name of the Lord!" Stephanie threw the holy water in Memphis's face.

The country-pop star's eyes widened, and she shrieked.

"You ruined my hair! Do you know how long it took to do this!?" Memphis's face turned murderous, and she headed for Stephanie.

"Mom?" Mary Beth appeared behind her mother. "What's going on?"

Memphis trained her eyes on the little girl. "Perfect. One more innocent I can take tonight."

"Don't you dare touch my daughter. Or I'll kill you." Stephanie looked over her shoulder. "Mary Beth, get out of here."

"No, Mary Beth. Stay. This is just getting good." Memphis smirked.

Stephanie's bravado slipped, and she turned to run but

skated on the wine Memphis had spilled on the floor. "I've already called the cops. They are on their way."

"You moron. I own the cops in this town." Memphis advanced on Stephanie.

I picked up the crucifix, surprised by its weight, and whacked Memphis over the head.

Memphis blinked and stumbled but didn't go down. I hit her again. This time, her eyes rolled back in her head, and she crumpled to a heap on the tour bus floor.

"Do you think you killed her?" Stephanie looked at me.

Memphis moaned and tried to move.

"No. But we need to get out of here now." I ran to my girls. "Stephanie, help me!"

"Oh, God. What happened?" Stephanie's looked at the bed where Gabby and Arianna were lying. "I knew it. I knew what Memphis was."

"You did?" I helped get Arianna to her feet while Stephanie and Mary Beth helped get Gabby.

"She's a child trafficker. She kidnaps kids and sells them to evil groups who sacrifice children to the devil." Stephanie nodded. "I knew it all along. But everyone thought I was crazy."

Mary Beth gasped. "Mom!"

I spun around to see what she was looking at.

"Dear God. She tried to sacrifice a man." Stephanie covered her mouth and took a step back.

"I know." I looked back at Khalan. "Look, I can't leave him here. Can you and Mary Beth take Arianna and Gabby back to my car? I need to help him get out before Memphis gets to her feet." I shoved my purse at Stephanie.

"But I can't leave you alone," Stephanie implored.

"Get the girls out. I need to know they're safe, Stephanie." I glared at her.

"Okay. Where did you park?"

149

"At the end of the world. It's the last row in the whole damn parking lot. When you get close, just hit the alarm. I'll be there as soon as I can. Now, go!" I turned my back on them, hoping Stephanie got the hint.

"We will wait for you at your car," Stephanie said over her shoulder.

After I heard Stephanie close the tour bus door behind her, I hurried over to Khalan. He was pale, paler than I had ever seen him.

His head lolled to the side. "What are you looking at, Road Kill?"

"Oh, God, Khalan. What did she do to you?"

"You need to get out before she comes in here."

"I can't just leave you like this. She'll kill you." Tears burned behind my eyes, and I touched his chest where she'd cut him.

"If I'm lucky, she'll kill me." He mustered a slight grin.

"I'm not leaving without you."

"As your Maker, I command you to get out of here," he growled.

"When have I ever listened to you?" I narrowed my eyes. "Now, shut up and tell me how to get you down."

He stared at me for a few seconds before he spoke. "You need to pull the nails out with the hammer." His gaze landed on the tool lying near his feet.

My stomach turned. But I had no choice.

I picked up the hammer. It felt very heavy in my hand, almost as weighty as my heart.

I swallowed back my revulsion at the task and lined up the claw with the nail.

I looked at Khalan. "I'll try not to hurt you."

"I've been hurt worse."

I tugged the nail hard several times before it finally slid out of both the wall and Khalan. I looked at him. Sweat had popped out across his forehead, but like a trooper, he didn't utter a sound.

"One to go." I set about my task again when pain raced through my back. I dropped the hammer and screamed. I spun around. Memphis had regained her strength and was holding a cleaver now dripping with blood. My blood.

"You little bitch. Do you think I'm going to let a woman come between me and Khalan? I'll cut you up into little pieces and glamour him into eating every little bit." She raised the cleaver, but I launched myself at her, knocking her back onto the bed.

Evil shined in her eyes, and she raised her hand with the knife.

I kept my weight on top of her and held her arm down so she couldn't cut me. She screamed and sank her teeth into my hand.

I pulled my hand away, and she bucked me off her to get the advantage. She straddled me and held up the cleaver.

Scenes flashed through my mind. The birth of my children. Parties and birthdays. Laughter in the back yard while they swam. Watching them sleep at night. Khalan carrying me in his arms while I cried.

"Let's see how lovely Khalan thinks you are without your pretty face," Memphis sneered.

A knife impaled her throat. Her expression changed to one of surprise and shock. She dropped the cleaver and reached for her neck. Blood bubbled out of her mouth and nose. The knife disappeared and then severed her head from her body.

Khalan stood behind her, holding up her detached head. A nail was still impaled in his wrist, and blood dripped from his wounds.

"I thought you couldn't kill your Maker?"

"You'd be surprised what you can do when you put your

mind to it." He dropped Memphis's head on the bed beside her body. "Let's get out of here."

"Not before we finish this." He grabbed some lighter fluid on his way through the kitchen. "We need to burn the bus. There's going to be a lot of questions if we don't."

He splashed the floor and bed with fluid and then lit a match. Fire danced to life.

"Let's go." He wrapped his bloody arm around me and ushered me out of the bus.

I was surprised that there was no security around. I guessed they were getting ready for the concert.

I looked over at Khalan. "We have to get you a shirt. You're sticking out like a sore thumb." We passed a tent, and I ducked inside. It happened to be a merchandise tent where they kept the extra stock. I rifled through some black shirts with Memphis scrawled on the front until I found an XL.

I ducked outside and shoved the shirt at Khalan. "Put this on."

He scowled. "No."

"Do it. Or I'll put it on you myself."

He lifted the shirt over his head and tugged it on. It was snug against his large body.

"I look like an asshole."

"You look like a fan, and you will blend in." I wrapped my arm around him, and we started toward the exit.

I held my breath, hoping no one would try and stop us or talk to us. We almost made it out before Ricky Spencer stepped into my path.

"Hey, sweetheart. I saved you a seat."

"I don't…"

Khalan punched him in the face. Ricky fell to the ground like a fallen tree. "She's already taken," he growled.

I pressed my lips together to keep from smiling.

CHAPTER 25

*S*tephanie, Mary Beth, Arianna, and Gabby were all waiting for us in my car.

"Oh, God. I was so worried about you." Stephanie jumped out of the car and hugged my neck. She looked over at Khalan. "Are you involved with Memphis and her business?"

"No, he's not, Stephanie."

"Then what were you doing in her trailer?" She didn't look convinced.

"He was trying to save Gabby and Arianna," I said.

Stephanie frowned.

"This is Khalan. He's my...friend." I almost said *"Maker"* but caught myself in time. "He actually got really upset that I let my girls go with Memphis. He had a bad feeling about her, as well. So, he went to find them. She was going to kill him to keep him from talking."

"I knew it!" Stephanie pumped her hand in the air. "I knew I wasn't the only one who saw her for what she was." She looked over at Khalan. "We need to get everyone to the hospital."

"Actually, it would probably be best if you and Mary Beth

go back to the hotel and get some rest. I can take everyone to the hospital to get checked out," I said.

"But I can't just leave you to deal with this." Stephanie's eyes grew wide.

"I'll help her. Besides, your little girl probably has a lot of questions for you. She looks frightened about everything that went on tonight." Khalan's voice was gentle and calm.

Stephanie blinked. She looked back at my Volvo. Mary Beth's face was pressed to the window, her skin pale, her eyes wide.

"You're right." My friend touched my arm. "Thank you, Rachel. For believing me. And for saving my life. If you wouldn't have been there, Memphis would have killed me. I'm sure of it. I saw the evil in her eyes." Stephanie hugged me hard. "I don't think we'll stay in Memphis. I'd rather just drive back home tonight."

"I understand." I smiled.

"It's okay if you need to talk later tonight. I'm always here for you." Stephanie motioned for Mary Beth to get out of the car. I watched as the two headed for their own vehicle.

Khalan walked over to the back seat and opened the door.

"What did she do to them? Will they be okay?" I asked.

"She didn't turn them if that's what you're asking. She was trying to spill their blood so she could find my exact location. That's when she realized that I had given the girls my blood before I left town."

"She said as much. Why?" I looked at him.

"I did it to keep track of you and them. I did it one night while they were asleep so they wouldn't remember. Thank God, I did, or I wouldn't have found them in time." He looked at me. "Don't worry. My blood won't hurt them."

"Do I need to take them to the hospital?" I brushed Arianna's hair out of her face.

"No. But I do need to glamour them so they don't

remember what happened tonight." He looked at me and waited for permission.

"Go ahead. But give them a good memory."

He leaned over Arianna and brushed the hair out of her eyes. "Arianna, open your eyes."

She blinked very slowly and met his gaze.

Khalan bent closer and whispered near her ear. Even with my vampiric hearing, I couldn't hear what he said.

He reached for the seat belt and buckled her in before moving to the other side of the car to Gabby.

He looked at me. "Go ahead and get in the car. I'll ride back with you to help you get the girls inside the hotel."

I nodded and walked over to the driver's seat and got in. The sound of approaching sirens made me jump in my seat. I craned my neck and looked out the back window. The flames from the tour bus were massive and could be seen from the parking lot. I turned the key in the ignition and started the car.

My gaze turned to Khalan, who whispered something in Gabby's ear and then, with the same care he'd shown Arianna, buckled her seat belt. He looked at me over my child.

"Don't worry. By the time the fire trucks get there, the bus will be gone. There won't be anything left of Memphis."

I nodded. I hoped he was right. Trying to live as a vampire in a human world was getting harder and harder as the weeks passed.

He climbed into the passenger's seat. I glanced at the wounds on his arms. I would have to think of some way to cover those up before walking into the Peabody.

"Go." He looked straight ahead.

My nerves were on high alert as I made the trip back to the hotel. We didn't speak. I snuck glances at Khalan and noticed that he'd laid his head back against the headrest and closed his eyes.

He was paler than usual, and his body had suffered a lot of trauma under Memphis's sadistic hand. I had no idea what else she'd done to him before I got there.

When we pulled up to the Peabody, the valet hurried to the driver's side and opened my door.

"Hello, Ms. Jones."

"Hello." I smiled brightly and handed him my keys. I opened the door to the back seat. Khalan was already out helping Arianna out of the car before I could unbuckle Gabby.

Gabby gave me a sleepy smile and wrapped her arms around me. I picked her up and carried her to the front entrance where the doorman held the door for Khalan and me.

Arianna had wrapped her arm around Khalan's waist and leaned against him as they walked. Something pulled inside my heart at the sight. Her long, dark hair covered up the wounds on his arm around her back, while she held her arm over his on her stomach. He looked like a loving father helping his sleepy daughter inside the hotel.

When we got to the room, I had to dig in my purse for the key. Once inside, I locked the door behind us and laid Gabby on the bed.

Khalan helped Arianna to the bed that Gabby was sleeping in and covered them up.

"I need to go." He rubbed his hand across his eyes and stumbled against the wall.

I hurried to his side. "You can't go out like this. You're not strong enough. Tell me what you need."

He leaned his head against the wall. "I need blood."

I frowned. "I can try to find someone in the lobby and bring them up here."

He shook his head. "No. It's too much of a risk. Not tonight. Not after everything that has happened."

"What about me?"

He frowned.

"What about taking my blood? I mean, when I was weak, you gave me your blood, and I have never felt better as I did after that."

"You don't know what you're asking." He looked away.

"What do you mean? What will happen?"

He turned his gaze on me. "If I take your blood, I will be more...connected to you than ever. You won't have your privacy."

"I don't have any privacy as it is," I deadpanned.

"You don't know what you're asking."

"Look, you need my blood. I'm giving it to you whether you like it or not." I grabbed his hand and led him into the galley kitchen. I braced my hands on the counter and hopped up and sat.

He stood motionless.

I grabbed his hand and pulled him between my legs. His nostrils flared, and his breathing became erratic.

CHAPTER 26

"*I*'ve taken too much from you already. I can't do this." He gritted his teeth. "Do you understand what Memphis was going to compel me to do? She was going to make me kill your children."

"But you didn't. You saved my girls. You saved *me*. This is the only way I can thank you." I held his hand between mine.

"Is it?" His gaze bore into mine. My body heated. Something shifted between us.

I brushed the hair away from my throat then wrapped my fingers around his neck and pulled him closer.

He didn't fight me. When his breath caressed my neck, he wrapped his hands around my waist.

"Don't let me take too much." His breath was hot against my flesh.

His lips pressed against my skin like a kiss, and then I felt a flash of pain as his teeth found their target. The pain bled away into pleasure. I trailed my fingers up his muscled arms and tangled them in his hair. He felt so right against me. His mouth sucked at my neck, and my flesh heated at the feel of him.

He tightened a hand on my waist and cradled my face like a lover with the other. I didn't even try to stop the moan that escaped my lips. He ground his erection against me, making desire pool in my stomach. I wrapped my legs around his waist.

"Khalan." His name escaped on a sigh. He moved his mouth from my neck and kissed the corner of my mouth.

I was dizzy with need and longing. He pressed his forehead against mine, and our breaths mingled.

"How do you feel?" I looked at him.

"Horny." His eyes burned into me.

I was, too. But I didn't need to say it. He read it on my face and in the way I rubbed against him like a cat.

He covered my mouth with his in a blistering kiss. His tongue slid against mine, and I could taste my own blood. It sent me over the edge.

I tightened my arms around him as he kissed me deeply. He tangled one hand in my hair and rubbed against my core.

I squeezed my legs around him. He picked me up and pressed my back against the wall.

"I wish you were wearing a skirt." He growled and kissed my neck.

"I wish we were in this room alone." I clung to him. Even fully clothed, he was giving me more pleasure than Miles ever had.

He rubbed against me until I came hard.

He covered my mouth with his, swallowing my scream. Fully satisfied, I wrapped my arms around his neck and laid my head against him.

"You need to rest." His deep voice sent chills against my flesh. He didn't set me on my feet but carried me bed and gently laid me down beside my girls.

He pulled off my shoes and looked at me before leaning over to unzip my jeans. I lifted my hips as he slid my pants past my thighs. His eyes darkened as his gaze landed on my black lace thong.

He straightened and laid my jeans on the chair.

I scooted over to make room for him in the bed.

"You can't leave. You need to rest. It's been a long night," I said.

He sat on the bed and tugged off his boots. He stood, and his fingers froze on the button of his jeans. "I'd better keep these on."

Disappointment tugged in my chest. But he was right. It wasn't like we could have full-on sex with my two girls in the room. No matter how hot and bothered we were.

I turned on my side, and he slid into the bed next to me. My heart thrummed in my chest at his nearness.

He'd just made me come, and yet here I was, yearning for more.

He wrapped his hand around my waist and tugged me against his stomach. I smiled and closed my eyes.

"Khalan?"

"Yes?"

"I'm sorry about what happened to your wife." My voice cracked on the last word.

"It was a long time ago," he said quietly.

Silence stretched between us.

"After you were turned, did you ever think about finding love again?" I found myself holding my breath.

"After what I have done, why would I deserve love? I killed my wife and unborn child."

"You were glamoured. You had no control over that." I looked at him over my shoulder.

When he didn't answer me, I turned over and met his gaze. "You are not responsible for what Memphis compelled you to do. She forced you into a life that you didn't want and turned you into…"

"A monster?"

"That's not what I was going to say."

"What Memphis did to me is exactly what I did to you. I took away your life. You had no choice in that." He rolled onto his back and covered his eyes with his arm.

Reality settled into my chest. What he said was true, but I didn't hate him like he hated Memphis.

"I don't hate you, Khalan."

"But every time you look at me, you are reminded of the life I took from you." He moved his arm and looked at me. This time, he looked tired.

"At least I still have a life. Let's just get some rest. It will be daylight soon, and the girls will be awake." I at my children. They were both in a deep sleep.

I turned on my side and waited for Khalan to snuggle against me.

This time, I was not disappointed.

CHAPTER 27

Khalan was gone when I woke up in the morning. I sat up in bed, oddly disappointed that he wasn't there.

"Mommy?" Gabby rubbed her eyes and looked over at me.

"Hey, honey." I hopped out of bed and sat on the edge of the mattress. "How are you feeling?"

"Okay. What happened last night?"

"What do you remember?" I brushed her hair out of her face.

"I'm not sure." Gabby frowned.

"I do." Arianna yawned and stretched. "Memphis wasn't who we all thought she was."

"What do you mean?" I froze. Had Khalan not glamoured her? Did they both remember that Memphis was a vampire?

"She's a sham." Arianna sat up in bed and frowned. "She said she was going to show us around her tour bus and entertain us, but all she did was yell and scream at everyone to wait on her hand and foot. She's not a nice person."

"And her songs aren't that great either." Gabby nodded.

"Do you guys remember anything else about last night?" I prodded.

"Just that she caught her tour bus on fire and the concert was canceled." Arianna shook her head.

Gabby grabbed the remote and turned on the TV. The news station was filled with the update on Memphis's canceled concert. The charred remains of a tour bus and crying fans filled the screen.

"Look!" Gabby pointed.

"The police are reporting that the decapitated body of the country-pop singer, Memphis, has been recovered from her burned tour bus. There has been speculation for some time that Memphis has been addicted to drugs and alcohol and some websites even say she is responsible for missing kids that have come to her concert. Certain websites have claimed that the famous country singer was involved in sex trafficking. Could this be related to the rumors of the darker side of the singer's life?. They are ruling her death as a murder and the FBI is now formally involved. ."

My mouth dropped open, and I looked at the girls. "I'm so sorry. I know you liked her music."

"I know I should feel upset, but oddly enough, I don't." Arianna looked at me. "I feel bad for her family, but it seemed like she chose that path, and that's kind of what you get."

"How about you, Gabby?" I looked down at her.

"It's sad when someone dies. But she kind of took her life for granted. And she didn't appreciate anything." She looked up at me and blinked. "Mommy?"

"Yes?

"I'm really hungry. Can we order room service?"

"Absolutely." I smiled and picked up the phone.

CHAPTER 28

*O*nce we got back home, Stephanie called to check on the girls and me. I told her that we were all well. She had seen the announcement of Memphis's death, and she said that she knew what had happened. She was convinced that Memphis had been killed by clients expecting to get children to sacrifice.

I didn't confirm what she said. I just told her it was plausible.

On Monday after I had dropped the kids off at school, I drove over to Uncle Stan's office. I still had the camera with the pictures of Carla and Jonathan. I hadn't decided what to do with them yet.

I didn't want to get Carla in trouble, but I needed this job.

I took the stairs instead of the elevator to give me some additional time to decide what to do. By the time I opened his door, I still wasn't clear on the answer.

"Rachel! Come in! I was just about to call you." Uncle Stan stood from behind his desk and waved me in. "How was your stay in Memphis? Did you enjoy the Peabody?"

"I heard there was some excitement." He stared at me as I sank into the chair.

"You did?" I swallowed.

"That singer was killed on her tour bus." Uncle Stan shoved his glasses on the bridge of his nose and leaned back in his chair.

"Oh, yeah. I saw that on the news." I covered quickly.

"So, I wanted you to come in here to talk about the case." He folded his hands across his stomach.

"Okay." I clutched my camera against my stomach.

"Jonathan Lender caught you taking pictures of him."

I cleared my throat. "Yes, well, I was trying to be discrete, and I thought he was with the bait girl, but it turned out he was with another woman."

"Another woman who was being paid for sex." Uncle Stan nodded.

"Yeah." I bit my lip. "Look, Uncle Stan, I think I messed up…"

"Messed up? You sure did." He slapped his hand on the desk and laughed. I jumped.

"I know they aren't supposed to know we are taking their picture, and I'm sorry about that…"

"I just heard from his wife, who is our client. And all I care about is making my clients happy so they can make me happy by paying me."

"Is she upset?"

"Upset? Hell, no. She's happy as a clam. It seems after her husband caught you trying to take his picture, he came home and agreed to give her a divorce and whatever she wanted if she just kept quiet about his activities."

"He did?" My mouth dropped open.

"He sure did. He is more worried about his reputation than staying in the church. So, we don't need the pictures." Stan nodded.

"You don't?" I breathed out a sigh of relief.

"Nope. And our client was so happy, she gave us a bonus. This is your take." He shoved an envelope toward me.

I picked it up and thumbed through the stack of hundreds. "Thank you. I thought I was going to be fired when I walked in."

"Fired? Not today." He leaned forward with his elbows resting on his desk. "But I do want to talk to you about Nikki's case."

I groaned.

"I may need you to work on it. More than just taking pictures. Is that going to be a problem?"

"Brad is dead. I don't know what I'm supposed to do to find a dead guy." Unease snaked around my throat. "I'm a photographer, not an investigator."

"I just need to know that you can do this job and not take anything personally. Even with the woman who fucked your husband." Uncle Stan stared at me.

"What do you want me to do?" I crossed my arms.

"Nothing yet. I just want you to be aware of what you might be dealing with. I need to know that you can handle it."

"I can." It might be a good idea to stay close to this so I could hide any evidence that would point to Khalan or me.

"Good. Now, go enjoy your day off. I'll give you a call when I need you." Uncle Stan stood.

"Thanks." I smiled and gathered my purse and camera.

This time, I took the elevator. When I got to my car, my phone rang.

"Hello?"

"Hey, Rachel," Miles said. "I heard what happened at the concert. How are the girls?"

"They're fine. They actually aren't too upset about it. I think their opinion of Memphis changed."

"Good. I don't know what they saw in her in the first place."

I sighed. "How's work going?"

"Good. You will be glad to know that I am out of the garage apartment and back in my condo."

"That's good. Sounds like things are looking up."

"Yep, they are. I just got a raise at the hospital, and I even bought a new car." I could hear the pride in his voice.

"Another Tesla?" I arched my brow.

"Nope. This time I got a Porsche."

My mouth dropped. All my goodwill toward him was waning. "I guess I can cash that alimony check now, huh?"

"Actually, if you could just hold off until after I get back from my trip to the Bahamas, that would be great…"

I ended the call and shoved my phone into my purse.

The two men in my life were as different as night and day. Both had destroyed their families, but only one was a selfish monster.

And it wasn't Khalan the vampire.

THE END.

ALSO BY JODI VAUGHN

THE VAMPIRE HOUSEWIFE Series
LIPSTICK AND LIES AND DEADLY GOODBYES (book 1)
MERLOT AND DIVORCE AND DEADLY REMORSE (book 2)
BULLETS AND BOOZE AND DEAD SUEDE SHOES (book 3)
ACES AND EIGHTS AND DEAD WEREWOLF DATES (book 4)

VEILED series
VEILED SECRETS (book 1)
VEILED ENCHANTMENT (book 2)

RISE OF THE ARKANSAS WEREWOLVES Series
BY THE LIGHT OF THE MOON (book 1)
BENEATH A BLOOD LUST MOON (book 2)
DESIRES OF A FULL MOON (book 3)
DARKSIDE OF THE MOON (book 4)
SHADOWS OF A WOLF MOON (book 5)
SECRETS OF A SILVER MOON (book 6)
FALL OF A BLOOD MOON (book 7)
RISE OF AN ALPHA MOON (book 8)
SHIMMER OF A CELTIC MOON (book 9)

CONTEMPORARY ROMANCE SERIES

Made in the USA
San Bernardino, CA
14 February 2020